Burton Harrison

**Belhaven Tales**

Crow's nest - Una and King David

Burton Harrison

**Belhaven Tales**
*Crow's nest - Una and King David*

ISBN/EAN: 9783337089184

Printed in Europe, USA, Canada, Australia, Japan

Cover: Foto ©Andreas Hilbeck / pixelio.de

More available books at **www.hansebooks.com**

# BELHAVEN TALES
# CROW'S NEST
# UNA AND KING DAVID

BY

## MRS. BURTON HARRISON

*Author of " THE ANGLOMANIACS," "FLOWER DE HUN-*
*DRED," "SWEET BELLS OUT OF TUNE," ETC., ETC.*

NEW YORK
THE CENTURY CO.
1892

THE DE VINNE PRESS

# CONTENTS

# LIST OF ILLUSTRATIONS

# BELHAVEN TALES

## L'ENVOI

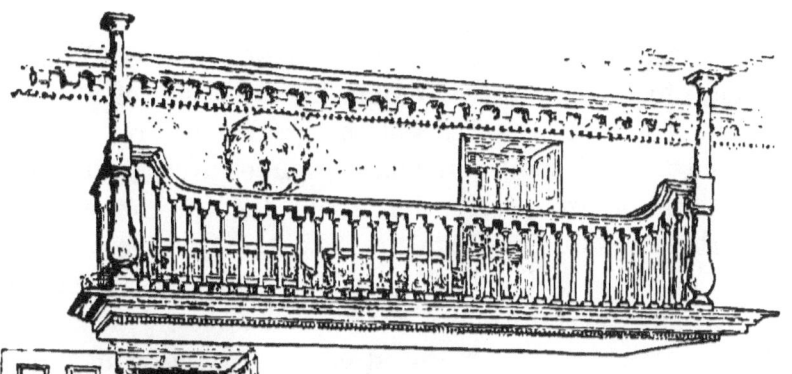

IN the quiet grass-grown town of Alexandria, first named Belhaven, situated upon the lower bank of the Potomac in Virginia, might have been perceived, just before the outbreak of the war between the States, a faint flavor of early colonial days lingering like the scent of rose-leaves in an old-time China jar.

To begin with the streets — what a Tory smack in their names! — King, Prince, Duke, Royal, Queen, Prin-

cess, Duchess. Odd enough in the neighborhood of
Mount Vernon—nay, under the very shadow, as it
were, of the great dome of the National Capitol! At
the time referred to, enjoyment for the greater part
of a century of the blessings of political enfranchise-
ment had not deprived some Alexandrians of a certain relish for the affairs of the English Court. They
liked to read the "Illustrated London News," and to
obtain correct information about the Queen's walks
with the youthful Royalties, and the Queen's drives
attended by Ladies X, Y, and Z. Had they not been
fed upon the traditions of an English ancestry, as upon
the toothsome hams, the appetizing roe-herrings, of
their famous market-place? The Georgian era of
tea-drinking and tambour, of spangles and snuff-
boxes, of high play and hair-powder, represented to
them the Golden Age in the fortunes of their families,
of which every vestige must be guarded jealously.
As children they had stood on tiptoe to study the
lineaments of great-grandaunt Betty, hanging in
her fly-specked frame somewhere near the ceiling,
and had been eager to hear how she had been toasted
at Mayfair supper-tables or had danced the gavotte
at a Ranelagh ball. Yonder beetle-browed warrior in
a voluminous wig was a general in Queen Anne's time,
before he condescended to his present station above
the sideboard. The beautiful youth in armor, slender
and graceful, with the fiery eyes, fought for King
Charles against the Roundheads, never dreaming that
he would come across the seas to find his niche in
a staid Virginian sitting-room! In this wainscoted
parlor, where the light comes through small greenish

panes of glass half veiled with ivy branching from stems knit in a fibrous mass upon the outer wall, had great-grandmamma, dressed in her satin paduasoy ("You may see a piece of it upon your Aunt Prunella's pincushion, my dear!"), her hose with silver clocks, stood to receive General Braddock, on the occasion of his first visit to the town. On the landing of yonder stairway little greataunt Nancy, the shy member of the family, while taking flight to avoid a sudden arrival of guests, had come into violent collision with Colonel Aaron Burr, who met her apologies with a smile and a bow treasured in the stronghold of her maiden heart through many a year to come.

In these echoing rooms had, from time to time, gathered all the celebrities of the day, coming to visit the haunts of Washington and to taste Virginian courtesy. And here, at a much later date, upon the occasion of his fourth visit to America, in 1824, was domiciled the gallant Lafayette. The tale of a famous reception tendered to that fortunate Frenchman is still told in the town. Escorted by citizens and militiamen, freemasons and Revolutionary survivors, the "Nation's Guest" passed along streets strewn with roses by the children of the place, beneath a triumphal arch the like of which in grandeur had never been seen. At the moment when the hero paused beneath the arch, a "real" eagle (politely furnished for the occasion by the proprietor of a museum) was seen to flap its wings, and heard to utter a scream of victory. This climax, it was afterward ascertained, was secured by a boy who, at the critical moment, stuck a pin in the bird of liberty. Bands played, flags and handkerchiefs were waved, salutes were fired. In the evening a banquet was spread at Clagett's tavern, followed by a levee. The market-place and many private houses were illuminated. Nothing was heard but honor to Lafayette. The wave of popular enthusiasm, overflowing to the rural districts of the interior, left inscribed upon more than one baptismal register the name and *title* of "Marquis de Lafayette," bestowed in a blaze of patriotic fervor, and in all innocence, upon the latest arrival in the family! At this day *"Marcus* D. Lafayette*"* remains guilelessly prefixed to not a few Virginian patronymics.

Then it was that Lafayette, before passing southward upon his pious pilgrimage to the tomb of his illustrious brother in arms at Mount Vernon, offered the toast: "The city of Alexandria! May her prosperity and happiness more and more realize the fondest wishes of our venerated Washington."

Even so early in the century the good old town seems to have been overtaken by the spirit of drowsiness from which the march of national progress has not yet aroused her. Long years ago, before the coquetry of fortune began to push poor Alexandria to her place among the wall-flowers, she had known better days. Founded upon the site of a trading-post by the Washingtons, the Fairfaxes, the Alexanders and other men of note, many prophecies were made as to her future greatness. Because of her natural position, her remarkable river-front, her dignity as one of the leading municipalities in Vir-

ginia, her connection with prominent families, all
eyes were turned upon the favored spot. From
countries oversea many settlers were tempted to
cast in their lot with the future metropolis. Mer-
chants of divers nationalities took up their abode and
displayed their wares in her aristocratic thoroughfares. Every sign foretold that Alexandria would
be quickly built up. Among the settlers was a company of Scotch traders; a band of Jacobite soldiers,
scattered after the battle of Culloden, also became
her active citizens. Soon the wharves were crowded
with shipping. Many a white-winged messenger
sailed down the broad bosom of the Potomac to
carry the products of bountiful Virginia to the
mother-land, fetching, on the return voyage, bricks
with which to construct the substantial mansions of
Alexandrian burghers, as well as carpets, porcelain,
furniture, carriages and wines. Inspired by the continual zeal and wisdom of George Washington, the
prosperity of Alexandria did not flag until the war
of the Revolution. Until Washington, unwilling to
be thought influenced in such a matter by his own
individual interest, selected the opposite bank of the
Potomac as the site of the National Capital, the little
Virginian town had every right to expect the distinc-
tion for herself. With this act of characteristic un-
selfishness on the part of the great Republican, her
dream of greatness came abruptly to an end, and at
Washington's death her mainspring seemed to snap.
What growth there has been since has been like
growth in sleep. To visit Alexandria, to-day, is to
see a wholesome brake set upon the rushing wheels

of nineteenth-century progress. Around her ancient homes and churches hangs a haze of dignified tradition. The cobblestones of her streets prate of figures famed in history.

In the treasure-house of the Washington Lodge of Freemasons may be seen many carefully preserved relics of the greatest of Alexandrians — notably, the clock taken from his chamber at Mount Vernon, its hands still pointing to the hour when he breathed his last. Here, also, are displayed portraits of Washington, of Jefferson, of Lafayette, and of Thomas, Lord Fairfax, the recluse of Greenway Court — this latter being the only known picture of a most picturesque figure upon the canvas of early Virginian days. Of this venerable lodge, a chapter of exceptional interest to antiquarians might be separately written. Unfortunately, the museum attached to the lodge and founded in 1811 was, after sixty years of existence, recently consumed by fire. Among the treasures it contained, then reduced to ashes or scattered to the four corners of our country, were flags carried by local companies in the war of the Revolution; the flag of Washington's life-guard; a collection of Indian relics of authenticated history; a number of portraits, including one of Martha, wife of Washington, in her girlhood; sundry Washington letters; card-tables and a settee from Mount Vernon; and various objects of minor value. The bier upon which Washington was carried to his tomb, the crape that hung upon the door at Mount Vernon to announce his death, and the military saddle habitually used by the great commander, long carefully enshrined in the museum, also disappeared on the occasion of the fire, but are believed by the authorities to have been stolen. Of the relics of Washington still remaining in possession of the lodge, now sealed behind glass in a niche of the main hall, are seen an apron and sash "worked by the hands of Fairly Fair"—the Marquise de Lafayette—and worn by Washington at the laying of the southeast corner-stone of the United States Capitol in 1793; fragments of the tent he occupied at the time of the surrender at York-town, and of the one he used on Dorchester Heights; his field-compass, farm-spurs and bits of clothing, etc.

Another landmark of old Alexandria is the house on Fairfax street, occupied for a time, through the courtesy of its owner, Major John Carlyle, by the British general Braddock, and since popularly known as Braddock's Headquarters. This square and substantial stone abode, where the chief scene of the "Belhaven Tales" is placed, once surrounded by a lawn stretching to the river-bank, is full of associations with colonial days. In its paneled drawing-room, early in April of the year 1755, General Braddock and Admiral Keppel held conference with the executive representatives of various colonies concerning plans for the proposed hostilities of the English against the French and Indian allies along the Ohio and St. Lawrence rivers. There were present five governors: * Dinwiddie of Virginia, De Lancey

---

* "Alexandria has been honored with five governors in consultation; a favorable presage, I hope, not only of the success of this expedition, but of the future greatness of the town; for surely such a meeting must have been occasioned by the com-

of New York, Morris of Pennsylvania, Sharpe of
Maryland, Shirley of Massachusetts. To meet this
honorable council, and to give them the benefit of
his knowledge of Indian warfare, Major Washington
was summoned from Mount Vernon. In spite of the
marked impression made upon the council as a body
by the young soldier's wise and moderate opinions,
Braddock declined to act upon Washington's advice
as to the best method of dealing with the Indians,
and the expedition against Fort Duquesne (from
which Washington did not withhold his own services
as an aid on the staff of the commander), setting forth
within the ensuing week, ended shortly in the fierce
battle of Monongahela, when Braddock fell, to be
buried near the field. It was in this bloody conflict,
it may be recalled, that an Indian chief, pointing
to Washington, cried to his braves, "Fire at him no
more. See ye not that the Great Spirit protects that
chief. He cannot die in battle!"

The Carlyle Mansion, miscalled by various writers
the "Jonathan Carey House," where the disastrous
campaign was planned, stands to this day, although
hemmed in and half shut from sight by the encom-
passing walls of an hotel. A pleasant picture has
been drawn of sundry occasions when Major and
Mrs. Carlyle received here their good friends General
and Mrs. Washington, who drove up from Mount
Vernon to "dine and lie" at Alexandria. The writer
retains, together with a bit of puce brocade flowered

modious and pleasant situation of the place, which prognosti-
cates population, and increase of a flourishing trade."—[*Washington's letter to W. Fairfax*, 23d April, 1755.]

THE CARLYLE HOUSE, ALEXANDRIA.

in crimson, green, and tarnished silver, representing
the glories of Mrs. Carlyle's gown assumed for a
Birthnight ball, a vivid impression of a scene preserved in family chronicle. The group of ladies in
the paneled parlor gather, splendid in trains carried
over the arm, lappets and pinners of antique mechlin,
powdered locks and superincumbent feathers. They
laugh and chatter, rally the general as to who shall
first claim him as her partner in the dance, and sip
their coffee from cups of jasper spode. The general
declares that his dancing days are over, but that he
must have one minuet with little Sally Fairfax of
Towlston, who is to go to her first ball under her
Aunt Carlyle's wing that night. Sally pirouettes,
laughs, warns her beloved general that her comrade
must be light of foot and tireless, then ends by chal-
lenging him to a trial of skill. Somebody sits down
to the spinet, and straightway the quaint measure of
the old-time dance is heard. The general lays his
hand upon his heart and bows. Sally curtsies de-
murely, her eyes full of merriment. They dance; the
others applaud. Suddenly, Major Carlyle looks in to
tell them that the hour has passed when everybody
was expecting the guest of the occasion to make his
entry into the ball-room; and the party scatters
hurriedly!

All good Americans should have, as all good Alexandrians have, a warm sentiment of reverence for
Old Christ Church. Ivy-clad and substantial, it
stands, save for the addition of a bell-tower, pretty
much as it was finished in 1773, at a cost of many
thousands of pounds of tobacco to the pious burgh-

ers, under a special contract guaranteeing to them
the best of English brick; mortar reversing the pro-
portion of meaner modern days, two thirds of lime,
one third of sand; and a roof of juniper shingles
three quarters of an inch in thickness. For so our
fathers builded better than we know!

Among the first pews of Christ Church sold in per-
petuity, was that for which George Washington paid
the highest price given. Thereafter, this pew was
a constant object of interest to the congregations
of the place, as indeed it is yet, being still carefully preserved and inscribed with the name of its
original owner. A treat to early Christ Church goers
was the arrival of the family from Mount Vernon,
sometimes a little delayed beyond the opening of
the service by the tenacity of Fairfax County mud.
Seated near her husband in the square, high-backed
pew was a gentle lady, still styled by the gossips of
the congregation "the widow Custis that was." That
same period, too, was made memorably sad by the
death, at sixteen, of the pretty, frail creature the
townspeople had been accustomed to see sitting on
the front seat of the chariot from Mount Vernon,
blushing like a rose in her coal-scuttle bonnet, and
like a rose, too, destined to endure but the "space of
a morning." Miss Custis, Mrs. Washington's daughter
of her first marriage, died in June, 1773, a short time
before the marriage of her brother John Parke Custis
to Miss Nellie Calvert. When Washington attended
service at Christ Church, in the pews around him
were gathered the Fairfaxes, Carlyles, Paynes, Alexanders, Herberts, Muirs, Flemings, Ramsays, and

others of the gentry of the region. It was the custom
of these good neighbors to assemble in the church-
yard, after service, to exchange greetings; and from
group to group went Washington, shaking hands and
answering inquiries till the patience of his wife and
that of the well-bred horses champing at their bits in
the street adjoining were alike exhausted. In this
quiet spot not a few of the friends then wont to assemble have laid them down to everlasting rest, their
names and virtues written upon gray slabs carved
with cherub heads and weeping willows, now blurred
with lichen and dark with weather-stains; and thither
have their children's children come to sleep beside
them. In the days when Christ Church was still subject to the jurisdiction of the Bishop of London, the
vestry had civil power to levy taxes, to bind out
apprentices, to make surveys, to receive fines for
broken game-laws. The rector's salary was paid in
tobacco, although we find recorded an award of eight
pounds (of money, not the staple weed) to one William Shakespeare for his care of a parish foundling.
Stories are still told of the two female sextons of this
church — one Susanna Edwards, and her successor,
Mistress Cook. Imagine a congregation of to-day
under the rule of an awe-inspiring dame who marches
up and down the tiled aisles, locking the pew doors
upon late arrivals, supplying prayer-books to the non-
devotional, and darting looks of ire upon hapless
Eutychus!

In walking through the streets of Alexandria, to-
day, one sees residences keeping up the traditions of
prosperous hospitality. Inclosed within high-walled

gardens, where the Southern sun coaxes from mellow
soil jasmines yellow and white, roses in prodigal variety, honeysuckle and all other sweet-smelling things,
the owners of these homes dwell year after year, un-
ambitious of change, gazing contentedly from afar
upon that "microcosm on stilts, yclept the great
world." It is the business quarters of the town that
strike most forcibly the visitor from one of the present centers of American commerce. From this old-
time seat of Virginian custom, the "fret and fever of
speculation" have forever fled. In the line of warehouses along the wharves, the quick "pulse of gain"
has ceased to beat. The vessels lying at anchor must
be haunted by ghostly crews; they give no sign of
life. The steamboat that plies her way between
Washington and Alexandria seems to approach the
wharf cautiously, as if fearing to awake a slumberer.
Even the fishing industry — for the beautiful river
has not ceased to yield her tribute — appears to move
but languidly. All this has its delightful aspect; and
he who would view a lotus-eater in his paradise should
watch an Alexandrian darky dangling his legs over
the worn beams of the dock under pretense of fishing,— listening to the lap of water against the green
and shiny piles, and droning away the livelong afternoon until the level sun, which gleams fiery red upon
the broken windows of the warehouse at his back,
begins to stir in him vague thoughts of corn-pone
browning on the cabin hearth at home.

Upon this background have been sketched the
stories following. Some of the incidents recalled in
them will be remembered by old Alexandrians. But

I have preferred so to blend my history with fiction that of the characters drawn none may be absolutely fitted to actual personages. A bundle of old letters, depicting the social life of Alexandria "when the century came in," was found, by a descendant of the young matron to whom they had been addressed, in a "huswife" of faded silk in a garret not long ago. These I have used in the first of my tales here following; and with the story they tell I have, while changing the names and suppressing many details, but retaining the general features, interwoven the love-episode suggested — a fact mentioned here to point what historical value the sketches may possess as a contribution to the sociology of earlier Virginian days.

NEW YORK, May, 1892.

# WHEN THE CENTURY CAME IN

## I

From Mrs. Ferdinando Berkeley, of Princess Royal street, Belhaven, near Washington, to her married daughter, Mrs. F. Faulkland, of Mount Eagle, near Charlestown, Virginia.

*3rd February, 1803.*

My dearest girl will, I know, acquit me of intentional neglect in missing the last post. At length, I have an opportunity to sit down and devote an evening to telling you our news; and, by good luck, the waggoner who is to take the bundle of linen and fustian I chose for you, will leave Clagett's Tavern to-morrow morning. Indeed, I could hardly rest last night for thinking my dearest Peggy might worry a little at not hearing from home, which would be bad for her and for my sweet precious new grandson — little rogue that keeps his mamma away from us, when her brother Billy is about to present his family with a Bride. To think, my dear, that your Brother's day is set, the seventh, next Tuesday! Oh! may the Almighty shower his blessings on the Pair. We — our entire household, except the little ones — are (if we are spared) to go over to Maryland to the wedding

14

—which is all very well; but, after a week's frolicking, the bridal party comes here; and then, Peggy,
pity me. Such nice managers the Stuarts are, and
old Mrs. S——, who will of course accompany her
daughter, famed far and wide for her housekeeping!
I shall be in a terrible pucker with them, and no
Peggy to help me with the whipt creams and drest
dishes. Ah! my dear, I owe your goodman a grudge
for taking you—the flower of my flock—away; but
there, I am not in earnest. I never think of your
match but with gratitude to God, and love to your
Partner. One thing only is wanting—were you but
near me—but the thought then strikes me that you
might have been as far removed and with an In-
different Husband; this reflection hushes all my
present regret. I am content, more than content, I
am happy—thankfull. Old Mrs. Stuart is vaunted
all over her State for her turtle-soup, and I need not
tell you, child—you have seen your good father pish
and pshaw over ours and push away his plate, often
enough—poor Penny is not at her best in turtle-
soup. However, if I have to sit up all the night before, and make some pretext to run out of the room
just before the dinner is announced, I will (if I live)
see ours rightly flavoured when old Mrs. Stuart
comes. Your sister Finetta, for a wonder, has come
down off her high horse and offered to make the
custards and jelly-cake. Little Jack says: "I wish
it were sister Peggy's jelly-cake," and I bid the child
run and play, for if Finetta heard that, away would
fly all our chances of a helping hand from *her*!

I almost wish I could stay away from the wedding

and have my mind at Ease for preparations. Billy
makes a point of my going, tho'; and, with Lucilla
and Finetta on the front seat of the chariot, and Tom
a-horseback, we are (if we are spared) to set out on
Monday next. But here am I, forgetting to tell you
why the affair is at the last so hurried up. You have
not forgotten that your future sister Juliana has enjoyed a fine name as a flirt, and has been blowing hot
and cold on Billy's flame for many months, & even
after she wore his Ring, wou'd never name the Day.
Poor Billy was too proud to let me know his suff'ring;
but who can deceive a mother's fond eyes? I saw
him mope at home, and then ride away to Maryland,
return more cheerful, & again fall into the Blues.
This was repeated, till I must needs take a tuck in
the back of his waistcoats, every one, and his coats
hung as if upon a rack. His beautiful hair went
rough, and his cheeks lost their roseate bloom.
Finetta gibed her brother, you may be sure, and
advised him to give up Prince George's County, and
look about him in Belhaven for a Fair. Next came
the rumour, just before Christmas, that Miss Juliana
Stuart was to wed with her neighbor, Colonel Crespigny, whom you have heard of as a great fortune,
the match of the county.

'Twill be never known what a time I had with Billy
then. Shut up in his room staring at the wall, or on
horseback riding so hard that he lamed the gray filly
which is not yet cured (and a pretty scolding he got
from your papa, who, Finetta says, in his heart thinks
the filly worth two Miss Juliana Stuarts!). At last,
Master Billy got the invitation to spend Christmas

week with Cousin John Thornton at Buck Ridge near
Annapolis, and fine doings they had. (I 'd warrant
Jack Thornton, for all his fifty years, to foot it with
the youngest beau in the party!) Pretty Miss Juliana
being one of the belles present, she and Billy made it
up; and Billy now vows Colonel Crespigny was never
more than a well wisher to his sweetheart, and that
it was ridiculous for any one to say otherwise. (He
forgets his own jealousy, my dear.) I must remark
to you, Peggy, that I did not think the Stuarts would
consent to the speedy marriage that Billy — methinks
wisely — insisted on. My son, although as everybody
knows the *handsomest, sweetest, dearest* young fellow,
the best rider and dancer in the town, has little beyond a genteel competency and his prospects from
your father's sister Ariana, now residing in the city of
Bath, England; & Miss Ariana Berkeley, it is equally
well known, is of a captious temper and apt to take
fits of changing her mind when least expected. Col:
Crespigny, on the other hand, has a fine old place and
manor-house, and his crops and negroes are prodi-
giously valuable, they say. Little Juliana, who is so
soon to be gathered to my Maternal arms, has, however, led her parents quite a Dance; and perhaps they
are pleased to see her safely settled. Little puss! She
has written to me a vastly pretty note, that makes
me forgive her coquetting with my Billy. And after
all, do we not every day see the greatest toasts and
flirts around us marry and make the best of wives
to those whom they have kept in suspense until the
very Nuptial Hour! You, Peggy, were not of that
sort. Never shall I forget your coming to me after

Mr. Faulkland carried off the ring for you at the Culpepper Tournament and courted you the same evening, saying "He is the only man I ever could have
chosen to be my lord!" Finetta is so sharp with her
would-be suitors, that I doubt me she will ever make
any selection; and little Lucilla is too young to
talk about beaux and weddings, yet a while, thank .
goodness! I must tell you, child, that Lucilla, at
fifteen turned, is beginning to improve mightily, in
shape and complexion. Billy and Tom declare she
will beat Sister Finetta hollow, but that none can
come up to Sister Peggy. If it were not for her un-
fortunate red hair, which alas! *nothing* can remedy!
I have kept Susan's Sally combing it for hours with
the lead comb; it has been wash't in medicated
waters; and yet it remains the same—brown in the
shade, but, when the sun strikes it, as red as the sorrel's mane. Cousin Priscilla Randolph, who has just
returned from Baltimore, brought us word that the
latest style there, is to wear the hair close and glossy
like a Sattin cap. Those Ladies whose locks will not
yield to smoothing with the brush, oil and pomade
them freely. Finetta, who always seeks the latest
mode, wore hers so to a party, last week, and I have
tried to persuade Lucilla that this is her chance to
hide the *defects of nature* at the wedding. I coaxed
her into the Chamber, recently; and made her stand
still, while I put onguents on her hair, and forced it
to lie smooth. At last 'twas of a rich, dark colour
that nobody would dream of calling by that odious
word *red;* and, for once, I breathed free about my
poor dear's appearance, when in came Tom from

riding, and laugh't at her, and cried out, " Little Lu's
head looks like the mahogany knob on your chest
of drawers, mother." Out ran Lucilla in a passion,
wash't her hair in hartshorn, & when she came down
tossing her locks like a Shetland poncy, I 'll own to
you, child, I gave her a smart scolding and bid her
take her own stubborn way. When my precious
grandsons (bless their hearts — I keep little Urban's
curl, till I can get a locket fit to put it in. You will
find a nice batch of horse-cakes and sugar-candy in
the bundle for him, with grandma's love) get big
enough to have their own way, you will understand
some of the trials of a mother's lot!

Here I am wand'ring away from the wedding,
which is to be a grand affair, the Stuart house full,
and every house in the neighborhood crowded with
guests. My Billy is in such a state, I hardly think
he knows whether he walks or flies, & Mother must
always be ready to hear his raptures. He has given
Juliana a set of pearls, necklace, brooch and spray,
and has bought the tiniest little ring, I protest
't would fit a fairy.

Oh! Peggy, what with ordering dainties and drill-
ing the servants, and keeping your dear father in
good humor about our large expenses, my hands
have been full. Of course you will want to hear first
about our dresses. I have got me a grave colored
Sattin, nearly puce, I will enclose a scrap to let you
see the colour — and with the old lace, it will have
to be first day's and second day's best, too, I reckon,
for there are Finetta & little Lu to fit out. Finetta
has bought herself a new White Lutestring — a lav-

ender gauze, a cross-barr'd Blue Lutestring, and two
new dimity frocks for morning. She has a beautiful
Rideding-dress near the colour of your Great Coat,
but a Casimer. She has some notion of getting a
plain muslin; she has made up her worked one
fashionably, & it is very pretty. The Ladies now
wear a Lace Veil and two Long White feathers in the
hair, the veil pinned up—a handsome head dress, and
the newest; so of course Finetta has one, besides a
wreath and bunch of flowers, & you see she is smartly
fixt. Tom vext her by saying she was going to set
her cap for Col: Crespigny, and Finetta bridled and
coloured furiously. Then saucy Tom said if Col. C.
knows what is good for him he will chuse little Lu,
who is so good natured she will let you pull her hair;
and I said "no more nonsence like that, Tom. I'll not
have Lu snatched up and carried off by a husband
like Peggy was, at sixteen!" Which I tell you, my dear,
repenting it, for if ever girl was blessed in a kind,
generous spouse 't is you; and well may old Penny
say: "Husbands like Marse Frank Faulkland don't
grow on bushes by de way." Lu is vastly set up with
two new white muslins over blue and pink silk slips,
and a white dimity with bird's eye dots of cherry. I
wanted a new pelisse for her, but the bills this year
will be so large I dare n't propose it, even to your
dear generous papa. You know he has taken a lease
of Clairemont for Billy and his wife. Since old Mr.
Mason died, the place has been in the market to rent.
Mr. George William Carter, who married Mary Turber-
ville, writ up from Westmoreland to have it pur-  .
chas'd for him; but the executors would not consent,

and Mr. Carter, 'tis said, is too Aristocratic to live on
rented land. My poor Billy, unless his aunt Ariana
helps him, cannot be so choice. There is a good
house, good water, gardens, ice-house, stable, poultry-
yard; I doubt if Miss Juliana, although she did not,
like you, have the bar of a town education, will raise
many fowls. Your papa kindly promises to do their
marketing for them, and you know what a fine hand
he is. They need only send a servant twice a week
to town, and Billy will keep up the farm, which is
small but in fair condition. I am gossiping on, my
Peggy, as if you were in the Chamber with your little
mother chattering in your ear. I must thank you,
love, for the pickles, the best I ever ate, and I am
proud of your getting over that trick of over-spicing.
I could always trust my Peggy to conquer her worst
faults. Oh! my dear, I drop into bed this night
weary but thanking the Almighty for my two children's blest lots. If I were to chuse through the world
I'd have selected dear Mr. Faulkland, and Billy's
happiness is mine. If Finetta could only curb her
tongue and temper a little bit (I know her heart is
right) I should have nothing else to ask. Tom and
Lu and the little ones are so well grown and good,
and no woman, not even you, Peggy, had ever such a
Partner as mine is. Kiss my babys for me. Finetta
will write directly after The Event. God bless all my
dear ones, prays their affect'te

S. BERKELEY.


P. S. Pray tell Harriet from me that her children
are well and in good places, and that she may trust

me to take care of them. My servants have been un-commonly well this winter, except old Dilsey, and a Doctor the old woman called on in my absence at your house, bled, blistered and salivated her so that when I returned she had hardly any pulse. I was obliged to give her a quantity of Madeira wine, and take great care of her & she is now hearty. Cousin Potts is about to try Electricity for her rheumatism, having exhausted all other remedies. It frights me to think of such a daring thing. Do, my dear, keep using the bark powder for your teeth—they were always extreamely delicate. Pray do not omit my affect'e Compts to your husband's Aunt Griffin, should she come to visit you, although, fortunately, the roads between you are so bad. I must not Cloase without telling you that poor old Mrs. Giddy died of a Con-sumption, and we have Lost our neighbor Mrs. Jones, who hanged herself, while deranged, by tyeing a handkerchief to a Tester of the Bedstead. Mrs. Rose has a Beautifull Boy, and would like the pattern of your darling nurseling's caps.

## II

FROM Miss Berkeley, of Princess Royal street, Bel-haven, to her sister, Mrs. F. Faulkland, of Mount Eagle.

23rd February, 1803.

Well, my dear Peggy, as we wrote you, the great Affair is over, and I take pen in hand to give you fuller particulars of an Occasion where you were sensibly mis't, and often reverted to, by Enquiring

Friends. The Stuarts gave a splendid entertainment,
all the rooms open and drest with laurel and crow's
foot garlands, wax-candles by hundreds, on the supper-tables a profusion of pine apples, oranges, cocoa-
nuts and other rare West Indian fruits, besides sweets
& oysters, crabs, salads, turkeys, wines and punches.
The greatest display of Glass and Plate I ever beheld.
(I wonder if any of it was borrow'd or hir'd for the
occasion!) The bride came down the stairs and joined
with Brother Billy at the foot, and the bridesmaids
followed, among them Lu and I, and walked in to the
big saloon and stood before the parson in a semi-
circle. They call our new sister a beauty, and beauty
she may be in *Prince George's*, but she is not up to
*Belhaven* standard, in my opinion! She has a little
pale face, and big dark eyes, and so much brown hair
it is too heavy for her head. Billy's pearl spray was
its only ornament, except a camellia behind one ear;
and she wore a plain square of Blond for a veil. Her
dress was white Sattin, of course—not as good a quality as yours, my dear, if that will comfort you — &
her figure is like thread-paper. We danced till morning, Brother Billy leading in the reel with his Bride
— my partner, Colonel Crespigny, whom you may
have heard of, a neighbor of the Stuarts, and a
monstrous fine young man. He asked little Lu, to
dance a minuet with him, to the child's great discom-
fiture, and I fancied her head would be *quite turned.*
Next day, there was a dinner for all the gentry of
the neighborhood. We sat down at three o'clock &
did not rise till six; the same profusion; & I thought
our little mother would feel put out of countenance

by Mrs. Stuart's table. But Lord! when you came
to taste the calf's foot jelly, it was poor stuff, I'll
warrant you! And the Blanc Mange eggs in the hen's
nest hardly seasoned, & half melted! The bride's-
cake was fine to look at, iced by the Confectioner in
Washington with a sugar Cupid in a Cage on top,
and a sugar couple standing before Hymen's altar,
under it. I took a bit to sleep on (they teased me
next day to know if I dreamed of *any Colonel*, but of
course that 's nonsense, child); and I broke off a
crumb or two to see what Prince George's could do
in the way of black cake. Bless me, Peggy, it was
not a patch on yours! The icing had *no orange-flower
water* in it — *no blanched-almonds* — conceive of such
a thing! And this they call the *model housekeeping* of
Maryland!

Juliana's second day's dress was pinkish lavender
brocade with pigeon bertha and ruffles of white silk
muslin. I wore my cross-barred lustring, and Lu
wore her other muslin. Papa, who, all the way driving over in the chariot, had fretted, vowing and pro-
testing he would leave for home the next morning
after the wedding early, as he could not abide jun-
keting among a lot of idle people, jok'd and told
stories, touch'd glasses with all the gentlemen, &
was the life of the party. *Between ourselves and the
Church clock*, he was in *no hurry* to get home! You
won't believe it, Peggy, our papa danced the reel with
fat Mrs. Stuart, and cut the pigeon wing — yes! and
a lively one. He skipped into the air!

Thursday, our Papa and Mama returned to Belhaven, but I was prevail'd on to stay, and they kept

little Lu because, forsooth, I suppose they feared me
being homesick. Col: Crespigny brought his horses
for me to ride; & on Friday gave us a dining at his
Mansion which is truly elegant. He is a tall dark
man, a little reserved in manner, a bachelor of two-
and-thirty. Any one can see 'twas merest folly to
talk of his caring for Billy's Juliana. Well, my dear,
to make a long story short, we stayed out the week,
and then bride and groom and wedding party came
over to Belhaven, our chariot sent again for us, the
rest riding or driving as they fancied. Col. Crespigny would have little Lu and me mounted on his
horses, while some of the elders took our places in the
chariot. It was clear, mild weather, a touch of Spring
in the air, and our ride delightful. (You must know
the Colonel, Peggy. He is about Mr. Faulkland's
hight and build, but less gay and off-hand than your
spouse.) Now, for the celebrations of the week. The
town is very gay, and I tell you we have no cause to
blush for Belhaven entertainments. A party every
night, abundance of costly viands, Mrs. Swann's supper being set forth on a new service of glass that cost
her three hundred dollars in Philadelphia; and Mrs.
Tyler's old English plate all on her table at once.
Oh! my dear, such an odd affair. Miss Kitty Dick-
son's wedding, of which so much has been said — the
town is in a Hubbub over it. A Thursday was the
day set, *but the bridegroom did not come!* The cakes
were made, the supper drest; everything ready but
the Gent'n, a very important part of it, *at Miss Kitty's
age*, especially. You may guess the gossip this occasioned. Such ridicule — such triumph in the Mali-

3

cious! Though that family are not my first favourites, it put me out of conceit with Human Nature. The bridegroom, Mr. Pearse, neither came nor sent word, and for days the Dicksons were in the uttermost perplexity. At last, *on the following Thursday, he* came, and with him his Sisters. It seems they *mistook the day!* And now, everybody flocks again to the house and the nuptials take place duly, Miss Kitty in—1st day—White Sattin & crape; 2nd. day—White Lutestring and muslin. At the 1st day's entertainment a prodigious company of married gents & Ladies. 2nd. day, all the young genteel people in the town. Both suppers were superb—pyramids three hands high, and everything renewed for the second supper. Mr. Pearse, about whom the Dicksons had so much pother, is, now they have got him, homely enough to scare the crows in his own cornfields. Rumor hath it that your old friend Louisa Beckwith is to marry Johnny Boyd, the little broken-backed man; there is no doubt husbands are scarce when little Johnny gets picked up. Almost every family of our acquaintance has called upon Mrs. Billy, and we have had four large dinner companies for them, and evening entertainments too, & they have been much invited out. Mama is on her feet greatly, but keeps in good health, and old Penny has done wonders in the cooking. Brother Tom was a subscriber to this year's Birth-night Ball, and he came off with great applause, every one seem'd pleased with his Gayety and Candour, though he speaks his mind so freely. Little Lu has contrived to see a good deal of the goings-on, spite of our intentions to keep her in. I confess the girl is much improved in looks. Peggy,

don't you — Honour bright — child, never feel that
you 'd give your ears to be back in all our gayeties,
instead of away off there mewed up with your husband and Babys in the country? You that was
lately so full of life and animation? Ah! well, child,
perhaps you 're right — (for I can hear you answer
"*No*") — Methinks I can sometimes understand it —
But enough of this — I have promised Col. Crespigny to ride with him tomorrow to Washington to
call on Mrs. Law. She is in the midst of the fashionable whirl, and I have seen her little. That city
was never so gay since the Government was fixt
there, but, for reasons you know of, we prefer Belhaven society. Our Papa, spite of his kinship with
the President, hath so strong a dislike to what he
calls Mr. Jefferson's scandalous low notions about
putting us all on a par with the lower classes, he will
not hear of our waiting on the Ladies at The Palace.
He and the other Federalists in town still feel deeply
the slight put upon the British Ambassador's lady at
the banquet in December, when the Presid'nt gave
his right and left to Mrs. Madison and Mme. Yrujo,
and forsook Mistress Merry to shift for herself! Nothing is heard discust in Washington, but the question of this or that official lady's precedence, and the
turmoil is fatiguing to us who *know our places*, and
fret not at *Imaginary Slights*.

Oh, my dear! Col. Crespigny is a *Republican*, the
friend and Crony of Mr. Madison, the Secretary of
State, and also of Genl. Smith, and M. Jerome Bona-
parte, whose young wife, late the beautiful Miss
Patterson of Baltimore, is producing such a sensa-
tion, politically and otherwise, in *Court* circles this

season. Imagine my fear lest the subject of Politics
should come up at our Board when Papa might not
be in a mood to keep the Peace. Tho' the Col. is
most kind and considerate, he can not know, nor can
we always warn him, that certain questions of States-
manship are to our Parent like a red Rag to the Bull.
I gave him a hint of this in telling him that our
Papa's Sister Ariana had removed to take up her
abode in England because of her objection to the
"filthy Democrats," as she is pleased to style certain
of our President's supporters, and he laught saying
the Ladies were ever virulent in *Party warfare*, though
not always certain as to their *Premises*.

And now, my child, Adieu. If I have succeeded in
amusing you by my talk, I shall not regret the time
thus spent. We have twenty people to sup here to-
night, and the card-tables out afterwards. Our papa's
friend, the good Chief-Justice Marshall, hath promised to ride down from Washington and lie in Princess Royal Street. I must hasten to assist mama,
who with the family, including our new sister, desires
to be warmly remembered to Mr. Faulkland and
yourself. I remain your Ever Attach'd

FINETTA BERKELEY.

P. S. Do not think I mean anything by my talk
about the Colonel. And pray, for Mercy's sake, don't
let Mr. Faulkland see this scrawl. Mama desires me
to add that, should little Urban catch the *Mumps*
(which, she says, may Heaven forfend), she hath a
wonderful new remedy of Dr. Dick's. Do not cut
your short gown by the pattern you took away, I
have a newer fash'n'd one for you. Little Lu hath

just run in to show me a nosegay of Cape jasmines and geranium leaves that Col. Crespigny hath fetched her from his glass-houses. You will say perchance that he is *most* anxious to please even this little one, but indeed, it is all in the fancy of the Gossips from whom our Society is not altogether Free.

### III

FROM Miss Lucilla Berkeley, of Princess Royal Street, to Mrs. F. Faulkland, at Mount Eagle.

6th March, 1803.

Dear Sister Peggy: I have been crying my eyes out, so that I can scarce see to dip my quill into the ink-pot; and yet I must write you, this post, because even our dearest little mama is not let into my room till I give up, and Susan's Sally has promised to get this letter to you someway, and oh! my Hart aches for you, Sister Peggy. Cou'd you but sit beside me on the sopha, and let me rest my head upon your breast, and tell you all, it would ease my pain I think. But, you will be wond'ring what has happen'd, unless (which is not likely) Mama has writ to you ere this. How shall I tell you, Sister, that I, your little Lu, the tomboy, the Red Headed Woodpecker as Bro. Tom calls me, have got a Suitor—a grand gentleman who has the ill-luck to displease our Papa in Pollyticks. (Mama says I am not careful in my Spelling, & I tried that word two ways but it does not yet seem right.) Ever since Bro. Billy's and Sis. Juliana's Wedding, I have known that the great Colonel Crespigny, who I danced with in the minuet, has been coming over

here to Belhaven to see poor little Me, for he told me
so, & I dar'd not tell Sister Finetta nor yet Mama,
for I fear'd their laughter.   He is so big and kind,
Sister, and his dark eyes made my Hart go pit-a-pat,
and it seem'd so great a thing to have a Suitor — and
such an one — before I was sixteen, that I kept the
secret close.   One day, when I met him on the Stairs,
and he whisper'd something in my ear, I went straightway to the old nursery, and put away my London doll
Aunt Ariana sent me (and which I nurst and drest
only a sennight since) till Baby Pen can be trusted to
handle it.   A week later, he came again, and when we
went from the Blue Parlour in to tea he slipped (in
passing) a bit of paper in my hand.   That paper burnt
a hole in my pocket, Sister, till I got a chance to light
my bed-room candle, and read it when I went up-
stairs.   I will write out what it said, for I learned it
by Hart, although Papa has sent it back to him.

### SONNET, TO ALMIRA.

The wand'ring exile on a foreign shore
　　By adverse fortune destin'd to remain,
　　Each long lost pleasure fondly traces o'er,
　　And sighs to tread his native soil again.
So I, when banish'd from Almira's smiles,
　　Nor crouded scenes, nor silent shades can please;
　　Fond Hope alone the tedious day beguiles,
　　Fond Hope alone, my drooping heart can ease.
Oft when I seek the solitary grove
　　Imagination holds her to my sight;
　　Or thro' the meadows pensive as I rove
When dark'ning shades proclaim the approach of night,
　　In fancy still, I gaze upon her charms,
　　And long with soft desire to clasp her in my Arms.

There, Sister, wou'd you ever believe that *I* am
"Almira"? 'T is so beautifully writ no copper plate
cou'd be finer; and where he tells how he seeks "the
solitary grove," it makes me want to weep for sympathy. But oh! I am not telling you the worst & at
any moment I may be told to snuff my candle out.
The last time the Col. drank tea with our parents, it
appears he had the ill-fortune to engage in an argu-
ment, Playful on his side, Heated on our Papa's,
about the Position (Sister Finetta said) of the President towards England. He took the President's part;
Papa waxed more and more scornful, shooting his
usual arrows of disdain at our Cousin Jeffn's habit
of dress, his slippers without heels, his ill-fit Cloathes,
his homely ways; Col. C. defending the Pdt. This
went on, till our Papa flew into one of his rages Wee
all know, and do not mind because they so soon Blow
By. Mama and Sister Finetta interposed, and led
Col. C. into another room, to hear Sister play upon
the harpsichord, but Papa has never forgot, nor for-
giv'n the Incident and its Cause. Yesterday — ah!
Sister, as I come to this, my tears brake out afresh —
My suitor came, arrived at the house & (so Mama
says) made a formal offer for my hand! Papa, most
polite and cold (you know how he can be, his wig
pushed a little crooked, his lips curling, his eyes like
blue steel), *refused*, without a moment's delay, and in
language so couched that Col. C., as a gentleman,
could but bow (though very pale, poor dear) & get
again upon his horse the groom was holding in the
street, & ride clattering away. I saw him from the
upstairs hall-window-seat (where I sat darning Papa's
silk hose), and tho' I did not know the reason, my

Hart misgave me all was over. Then Papa sent for
all the family — the elders I mean — in the chocolate-
panelled Study where his books stay, & told me I
must never think or speak of Col. Crespigny again.
Then I burst into loud crying and flung myself in
Mama's arms, who was trembling there, looking with
her pitiful kind eyes at Papa, and I vowed I would
love the Col. and none other, till I die. At which,
our father rose, and ordered me to keep my bed-room
till I knew myself for a headstrong impertinent little
Baggage, & was ready to ask his pardon and promise
what he required. Next, a strange thing happened,
Sister, that I cannot understand. Sister Finetta,
whose face I chanced to see grow red, then pale and
stern, stept out from the rest, and put her arm
around my waist. She that never caresses anyone!
She led me away up to my room, and kissed me in
silence ere she shut the door. Next, Mama came in
and, crying, told me it was all a sad business, sadder
than I knew. That she too (altho' not for my father's
reasons) counsel'd me to give Col. Crespigny up.
That, until I promised, she must leave me to myself
— and then she kissed me like the Angle that she is,
and went out and lock't the door. Without supper
(wh. I could not eat), I cried myself to sleep. To-
day I ate a mouthful of the breakfast brought me
by Susan's Sally; and since, I am writing this to you,
that I begun last night and writ till cautioned by
.Papa's voice outside my door, to go to bed. Sister
Peggy, you will (I know you, I can hear your gentle
questions that always made us confess everything)
inquire if I am *sure* of my own feelings for Col. Cres-

pigny, I that was a child when you saw me last.   In
answer, I say, "ask Yourself what if they had wanted
*you* to give up your Francis after that night he
Courted you?"   Yes, I do love him, I shall always
love him and honour him before all men.   I would
follow him to the Land's End, I think.   And—there's
some one coming up the stairs — oh! write to them,
Sister, you that can move papa if any one.   The person —'t was a servant asking if I would have refresh-
ment (I know the little Mother sent up those iced
maids-of-honour of which I usually ask for three, but
I cannot swallow now) — has gone, and I resume.   A
little while ago I took down from the shelf the sweet
Annual, bound in pink-and-gold — "Affection's Offering" — that you used to read in Company with Mr.
Faulkland during your betrothal.   Strange, passing
strange, that it should have opened at these lines!

With plaintive courage, lo! the turtle dove
Laments the fate of his departed love.
His mate once lost, no comfort now he knows,
His little breast with inward anguish glows,
Nor lawns nor groves his throbbing heart can charm
Nor other love his languid bosom warm;
Oppressed with grief, he yields his latest breath
And proves at last his constancy in death;
A proper lesson to the fickle mind,
An emblem apt of tenderness refined,
Affection pure and undissembled love,
Which absence, time, nor death can e'er remove.
Then like the dove let constancy and truth
And spotless innocence adorn your youth;
In every state the same blest temper prove,
Be fixt in friendship and be true to love!

Sister, as I write these words, so applicable to my condition, my tears refuse to be staunched—Oh! Sister, what shall I do—pity me, help me. Could you but come—but what do I ask, considering the Distance, the State of the Roads, your Young Infants, etc. No, I must be Brave. Write then, and I await your Counsel—but remember, I *cannot* resign my noble—my manly C. Do you think, perchance, he could be induced to become a Federalist—In truth I cannot see the difference between them and the Others Papa chuses to despise.

Yr. ever loving and afflict'd.

L. BERKELEY.

P. S. I believe I could promise that he would make no further allusion to the Presid'nt, or to England.

I broke off here, to receive a visit from my dear and honoured Mama, who came at the wish of my Papa—he having slept well and re-considered his Action of last night. Oh! dear Sister, you would never believe what our parent has convey'd to me. I dare not commit it to paper lest the Curious shou'd chance to read it—let Peggy who knows us all, divine—but I am now convinc'd that in fixing my affect'ns ou Col. C, I am wrouging Another—one innocent of Intention, a Victim of Circumstance. As by a Lightning-Flash, I saw what my self-willed determination to have my own way in this matter would entail. Immediately, I sought out my Papa, who was sitting, as Before, in the little chocolate room, reading a Journal which I observed to be Upside Down, while his hand shook, & his eye when he turn'd it upon me was velvet soft and loving. Our blessed mother went up to him, and with an arm around his neck, placed my hand in his. "Our child is worthy of herself, husband," she said in the sweet voice that sounds ever like a flute. "She hath promised to renounce what will cause more unhappiness to others than it can, now, bring happiness to her." Oh! Sister, when our parents gathered me into their Embrace, I felt like the Lamb that has been Lost and Found again—I can not now write more! Forget what I have said that was foolish or headstrong. Love me always, and believe that I will be true to my promise to Papa, and only you shall know what it Costs me to submit.

Your L.

## IV

From Ferdinando Berkeley, Esquire, of Princess Royal Street, Belhaven, to his daughter, Mrs. Faulkland, at Mt. Eagle.

11th October, 1803.

MY DEAR: I shall send this under cover to your good husband that he may consult his Judgement about delivering it to you or No. I conceive that the tenderness of the female nature, nay my Peggy's nature in especial, will make as severe to endure what I have to communicate, as 't is cruel to me to write it. My child, the Almighty hath laid a heavy hand upon our once happy household. The news-

papers will have informed you of the pestilential
fever that has mysteriously appeared in Belhaven.
As I was in the act of preparing to send my family to
the country, I meant to forbear writing to you until
they were safely away. But God's will be done—
your dear mother is laid low with the pestilence, and
2 of the servants, as well as your brother Tom. The
children, I have sent out to my son William's seat,
Clairemont, where Juliana will take faithful care of
them. Finetta alone remains in town, for Lucilla,
although most unwilling to be parted from her mother, has also gone, by my express command. Finetta, at ordinary times so difficult to controul, has
now, I am pleased to say, developed a spirit of help-
fulness and courage that makes her Invaluable to
her poor mother. There is so much misery attending this dreadful Calamity in the town, that while
my dear ones continue to hold their own, I will not
repine against the decree that has smitten us. My
Dr. Girl may Join her prayers with ours for the
preservation of our sufferers. I can write no more
at present. My Compl'm'ts to your Spouse. Lucilla
will keep you inform'd, or William or Juliana, as the
malady progresses.

From, my dr. Margaret, your loving and anxious
Father,

F. BERKELEY.

Pray inform your faithful Harriet that her children are well.

V

From Miss Lucilla Berkeley, at Clairemont, to Mrs. Faulkland, at Mount Eagle.

18th October, 1803.

God be praised, Peggy dearest, that our little Mother is said to be on the mend. Tom has been very Low, but he and our Mama owe their lives under God to Sister Finetta's care. Oh! that I were suffer'd to be with them, to be of service. I, whose poor life, clouded by disappointment, is of so little use to anyone. While our family is passing from under the pillar of cloud, people have dyed all around our house. The burials are frequent, the streets deserted. Marks of distress and depopulation on every side. If 't wou'd please God to send a heavy rain and severe frost after it, perhaps it might be checkt. What a mellancholy situation is our poor friend Mrs. Cracroft's; she has lost, poor Lady, both her Husband and her Daughter, Miss Betsey. What will be the end! Our hopes give way to Apprehensions, and yet Mama is better, and Tom is out of danger, and the two maids are improving. Thank you, Sweet Sister, for the last letter about my own affairs, that seem little now, beside this great Public calamity. I have bowed to my Earthly Father's, as to my Heavenly Father's will, but *he whom you know of* (so Juliana has heard from Maryland) has not ceased to hope that *affairs may change* in his Favour. Ah! what a selfish girl am I, to write of this now. Forgive me, Sister dear. Write to me

4

again. Brother Billy and Juliana and our children are well as can be. Tell Harriet hers are well, and I am your affectnte.

LUCILLA.

I open this to say a messenger has come from town. Bad news, alas! Sister Finetta, the Brave and strong, has been stricken down. I will keep the letter open till tomorrow to tell you what betides.

Tuesday morng.

Sister Finetta very ill, our mother still mending. Tom, poor brother, has a relapse.

I must Cloase to catch the post. The Doctor says Sister F. has it in a worse form than any of the rest. God pity us all!

L.

VI

From Mrs. William Berkeley, of Clairemont, near Belhaven, to Mrs. Faulkland, Mt. Eagle.

25th October, 1803.

My dear Sister Margaret will comprehend when I tell her that I feel my inadequacy to fitly represent the cherished members of her family whose place I assume to take in Writing this. My own Mr. Berkeley hath gone for a ride upon his bay mare to get rid (so he says) of the blue devils in his brain. He began a letter to you. But his fingers were all thumbs, and he gave up the task. Never have I seen his cheerful Countenance so overspread with gloom as since rendering the last sad offices to his departed brother Tom. That amiable and estimable youth will indeed be deeply mourned. We can but trust that he is now happy in the enjoyment of the everlasting felicity of Heaven. Your Beloved Mother, spite of her trials, continues to improve. And, God be praised, Sister Finetta yesterday (it is hoped) passed the turning-point of her malady, and will now recover. Beneath these encircling Clouds of Gloom it is my pleasing duty to inform you of the unexpected happiness of our little Pet, Lucilla, whose rare sweetness and beauty hath endear'd her to me as to all that know her. When your Sister Finetta lay (as it was believed) upon her death bed, she called your Father to her side & in feeble accents pray'd him to grant her the boon of withdrawing his Opposition to Lucilla's Alliance with Col. Crespigny. This, upon the assurance from me (who was fortunate to be so far in the Col's confidence as to bear proper witness) of his unaltered fidelity to the lady of his Love, was freely and tenderly granted by your Papa, which promise, 't wou'd seem, afforded at once to the sufferer a Calm, proving to be the precursor of Healthy Sleep. I have myself writ the summons to the Anxious Lover to meet Lucilla under her Brother's Roof. And if you will pardon the selfish thoughts of personal joy at such a Time, I would fain be first to convey the news that our Aunt Ariana at Bath, England, hath presented your brother with her handsome dwelling and estate, Shannon Hill, twenty miles hence

in Fauquier County, whither we shall in due time remove, and your brother be releas'd from the discomfort of rented land, which he has borne in silence, as befits his noble self. Trusting that the white-winged Dove of Peace and Happiness will henceforth unfurl her wings upon our Family, & with mine and my Mr. Berkeley's most affect. respectful Compl'mts to your husband, and kisses to your Pets, believe me,
Your attach'd, faithful friend and Sister,

JULIANA BERKELEY.

## VII

## A FRAGMENT

From Miss Lucilla Berkeley to Mrs. Faulkland, Mt. Eagle.

CLAIREMONT, 28th October, 1803.

Sister mine, my heart overflows in these few lines to tell you that He has come. Am I wrong, amid all the sorrow still ling'ring o'er my home and dear ones, to be so hap—

## PENELOPE'S SWAINS

IN the breakfast-room of the Misses Berkeley in old Belhaven town, in Virginia, you might, before the war, have beheld daily a pleasant spectacle.

As soon as the last relay of batter-cakes had been carried out by Trip, it was Miss Penelope Berkeley's custom to call in a black woman bearing upon a tray a cedar piggin hooped with brass and full of boiling water, a mop, a bit of soap, and some fair towels of linen crash. Into this tub the old lady would first dip her tea-pot, sugar-dish, and cream-jug of oval-shaped colonial silver; after them, in regular routine, cups and saucers, spoons and forks. Transferred from their steaming bath to Gay's dainty finger-tips, the various articles were dried and in pristine luster re-niched in a corner cupboard. Not for the world would Gay have let fall one of those family treasures. Her care for them was that of the Guards in the Tower of London for the regalia of the Crown.

One beautiful May day, when the custard honey-suckle had sent a flower inside the sash of the break-fast-room window to woo Gay into the garden, it was made evident by sundry tokens that something had stirred the spinster household from its normal calm. Trip, the kitchen Mercury, in a clean check pinafore, his head bristling with twigs of plaited wool, dis-played a continual grin and a pair of wildly goggling eyes. Dennis, the purblind butler, shuffling around the table, with snow-white jacket and long linen apron, wore an air of gratified hospitality, tempered only by the memory of Trip's shortcomings (Trip, his great-grandson, in training for house-service, was the thorn in Dennis's side), and Susan, the housemaid, had tied her kerchief with coquettish consciousness about her head. Upon the forsaken table, await-ing Miss Penelope's regenerating touch, was not a portion but all of the Berkeley tea-service (even the urn with a pine-apple on top, reserved for special tea-parties), and also the Nantgarrow cups and saucers, with brier-roses and trefoils, that saw daylight only behind glass, except as a mark of honor to cherished guests.

Gay, divided between her anxiety to see china and silver back in safety on the shelves, a physical excite-ment inspired by delicious weather, and a keen femi-nine relish for a sentimental situation, was in high feather. An old lover, a has-been suitor, who had sighed in vain and ridden away to come back after many years,—a widower, no doubt hoping to be con-soled—here, under the same roof with his first love— Gay an eye-witness to the progress of events,—what an enchanting combination! True, it had been something of a drawback to see the Reverend Dr. Fountain accept from Aunt Penelope's own hand three cups of coffee and a glass of milk in quick succession. He had also partaken more heartily of rice-cakes, waffles, rolls, light bread, batter-bread, cold ham, roe herrings, radishes and broiled tomatoes than accorded with Gay's theory of allegiance to the past or present of sentiment. She could not help wondering if the late lamented Mrs. Fountain had been what was called in Belhaven a " good provider."

And now that the meal was over, Dr. Fountain had retired with Aunt Finetta into the paneled parlor looking out across the garden and river to the red clay hills of Maryland. The door had closed behind them. Aunt Finetta, who invariably sat here in the family room reading her newspaper until the things were washed and put away and Penelope was ready to go to market! How funny it had been to hear the old lady say, with majestic courtesy:

"We will adjourn temporarily to the drawing-room, Dr. Fountain, if you please, leaving to my sister the care of our few domestic duties."

Was this, Gay wondered, a blind to give the doctor an opportunity to declare his enduring passion for Aunt Penelope, and to receive her elder sister's blessing on his hopes? For Gay had often heard the Belhaven gossip about the Misses Berkeley; how young Fountain, as a prospective clergyman, had been Miss Finetta's choice for her sister, and how Aunt Penelope had obstinately preferred that rattle-brained Daisy Garnett. Fountain, ordained a priest and called to a distant parish, had married and flourished and acquired a good-sized family, had now lost his wife, and was talked of as on the way to become a bishop. When it was announced that he would certainly be present at the annual convention of the Church, to meet that year in Belhaven, Aunt Finetta had forthwith invited their friend of olden days to be one of the two guests assumed as her share of town hospitality toward the clergy. This, to Gay's active mind, was a suspicious circumstance. She tried, but without success, to adjust to it some of the situations in the novels of Mme. d'Arblay or Miss Porter, dear to her through many readings in the hall window-seat up-stairs. Mme. d'Arblay had no elderly hero with a large purple face, shaven except for a beard like a goat's to adorn his chin, an oratorical style of general conversation, and a habit of blowing his nose with a resounding blast. Gay's idea of a lover was that he should use his handkerchief only to mop beads of anguish from his brow when unsuccessful in his suit.

In the sixteen-year-old judgment of a head stuffed with old songs, old sayings, old love-tales and young whims, there was quite as much incongruity with romance in the appearance of her aunt's other admirer of langsyne. Major David Garnett, yclept by his fellow-townsmen "Daisy," had been a famous Belhaven buck in the days when Birthnight balls still held their vogue. How often had Gay seen the pink satin frock, with its umbrella-gores and leg-o'-mutton sleeves, in which Aunt Penelope, at fourteen, had danced down the middle of a reel with Daisy, to

IN THE HALL WINDOW-SEAT.

wind up a Twenty-second-of-February ball at Gadsby's tavern!

"I was slighter then, my love," Miss Pen would
say when Gay's reverent fingers measured the width
and depth of the corsage. "I remember so well
this was new just when 'stooping' had been declared out of fashion. Dear mama made us wear
a piece of Russian sheeting under the bust, with
shoulder-straps, and brother Billy laughed and said
no fine lady but would now be seen bridling up
in company; and so it was. We wore our hair
smooth and glossy, like a satin cap, and on top two
or three bows of hair with feathers and roses. Mrs.
Betsey Thompson, who 'd been a widow just one
year,—she that was afterward Mrs. Colonel Steptoe,
of the Eastern Shore,—appeared that night in a
high black crape puff with silver spangles and
black feathers on her head, a frock of blue Italian
muslin, and a black spencer; this she was pleased
to call second mourning! The Misses Delaney were
the belles; they wore white lutestring with gold
spangles and gold cords, and green velvet leaves
sewed all round the tail—poor Billy was so attentive
to the elder, Sally Delaney, who married a Tucker
and died before my dear brother—where was I,
child?"

"At the ball, Auntie, dancing the reel with Major
Daisy. Tell me some more about the ball."

"There were seven hundred guests, my dear, and
the supper was truly elegant. I walked in the procession with Mr. Garnett. There was a monstrous
cake in the middle of the table, ornamented with an

equestrian statue of General Washington, the whole covered with sugar-candy in the form of a cone, on top of which was the American eagle. Then there were jellies and blanc-manges, oranges and nuts, all sorts of dressed dishes, ornamental cakes and sugar emblems, and the sweetest baskets made of macaroons and filled with kisses."

"Goodness!" cried Gay.

"Yes, there was no scrimping in those days, I'll promise you, though I *have* heard mama tell how the General used to laugh at some of the older Belhaven parties, calling them bread-and-butter balls. After the supper was eaten, the beaus scrambled for the sugar eagle on top of the cake, and Mr. Garnett got it and presented it to me."

"To think you were only fourteen, Aunt Pen, and I'm not allowed to turn out yet."

"It was the custom of the day, my love."

"What became of the sugar eagle, Auntie?"

"My child—some things are very mysterious. It crumbled away the year Mr. Garnett went to the war in Mexico. I opened the box to look at it, and found it quite destroyed; and the very next week came news that he was wounded at Chapultepec!"

Gay, who knew every word of the recital, always drew a long breath of awe-stricken satisfaction at this point.

There was no doubt that Miss Penelope, who could now speak of her old swain so calmly, had once wished to marry him. But Miss Berkeley, ruling her family with a rod of iron, would have none of David Garnett. She considered him a reckless

young fellow, unfit to be trusted with the happiness of her sole surviving sister, the youngest of the
flock.   Pen was inclined to giddiness, and Daisy far
too fond of frolicking, tippling, horses, cards, and
dancing.   One heard of him here, there and everywhere in Maryland and Virginia, at "weddin's," fox-
hunts, races and barbecues.   Worse than all, he had
exchanged shots in an encounter near Bladensburg
with a senator from South Carolina, with whom
he had had the misfortune to differ on a question
of State precedence.   After this, Miss Berkeley—
who, having once published a diatribe in pamphlet
form against the appearance of certain of the Virginian clergy in the chancel without robes, was considered to have a scathing style in authorship—sat
down and wrote to David, forbidding him the house.
Then it was that Penelope was said to have bowed
before the blast, and renounced the "understanding"
between her lover and herself.

Gay could not reconcile these traditions of Major
Daisy's *jeunesse orageuse* with the trig little lame gentleman wearing a rusty auburn scratch, his winter-
apple face crisscrossed with wrinkles, who, as regu-
larly as Saturday night came around, hung his hat
on the spinsters' hall peg.   Thanks to time, the soft-
ener of all asperities, Aunt Finetta defied David no
longer.   There was even a neighborly welcome for
him in Princess Royal street, where the old Berkeley mansion reared its high-shouldered chimneys
draped with English ivy and wistaria to the gaze of
passers-by.

Gay, taking part sometimes with the major and her

great-aunts in a four-handed game of cards, used to
wonder could this be the gallant volunteer who, when
left badly wounded by the tide of battle sweeping up
the heights of Chapultepec, had lain hugging to his
breast the flag he had snatched from the hand of its
dead bearer, and cheering his comrades on to victory? The major, whose game leg was a souvenir of
that occasion, had indeed long since settled down
from the ways of his wild youth into a Belhaven
landmark as steady and familiar as the town clock.
He had "joined the church" and become a vestry-
man; he was the leader in "Mear" and "Federal
Street" in a straggling choir of volunteers; was
frequently called on to be a godfather; and as a
pall-bearer was an assurance to survivors of the
high respectability of the departed.

It was a common saying that no wedding could
take place without "points" from Major Daisy.
First to know of the engagement—what time the
bud of love had been pleased to break into unex-
ampled flower—he was the confidant of Jenny's pets
and Jessamy's despair, and in due course brought the
lovers in safety to the altar, gave away the bride,
and was the first to salute her blushing cheek. At
the wedding-feast who but he could be counted on to
offer toasts, fill plate and glass for lonely wallflow-
ers, lead out touchy maiden aunts, joke with "the
boys" who wore the willow for the bride, and keep
the bridesmaids in a flutter with his compliments?

At christenings Major Daisy was great. He had a
genius for discovering in the unformed features of
the infant on exhibition the likeness of all others it

was meet and right for that child to have. Was there in the family annals a distinguished dimple, or scowl or squint desirable to perpetuate, he would espy and proclaim it to flattered parents.

At funerals, again, he might be seen, his hat borne down under a long black weeper, his hands lost in the wrinkles of undertaker's gloves, walking in the procession with a look of rooted gloom. Thus equipped, he inclined bystanders to believe in the great loss the community sustained in the death of old Aleck Appleby, who for twenty years had been soaking himself in whisky and disgracing all his kin.

In politics Major Daisy was an old-line Whig, contributing, over the signature of "Senex," many articles on the tariff and subjects of kindred interest to the columns of the "National Intelligencer" in Washington. He was, in theory, a deadly opponent of some of the incendiary teachings of Thomas Jefferson, and his modern idol was the Honorable Henry Clay. He was an enthusiastic freemason, frequenting the lodge of Washington in Cameron street; and as a citizen was second to none in the estimation of his townspeople, although not in active business, having inherited a wide old double house in which he lived alone, and sufficient patrimony for his small wants and large charities.

Ah, yes, it was years since Miss Penelope had folded away her love-dream, sprinkled with rue and pansies, like a garment of the beloved dead. And yet little Gay's sharp eyes were not mistaken in seeing upon her faded cheek a faint warmth when the

5

major stepped in on Saturdays to offer her revenge
at cards or chess or backgammon. He brought her a
pink rosebud once, plucked in the yard while waiting
for Dennis to hobble to the door—and reminded her
that she had always looked so well in pink. Next
day Gay found Miss Penelope picking out the
rosettes of lavender "love" ribbon in her evening
cap and fumbling with some loops of rose color.
But Miss Finetta's brusque entrance and demand to
know what nonsense she was at, fussing with such
colors at her age, made Miss Penelope hasten to
put back the lavender, which had never since been
changed.

Miss Penelope Berkeley was now a fair, pretty old
lady, with dimples and a double chin, her drab hair,
once golden, worn in two "sausages" on each temple.
She had grown stout, but was still active on her feet,
and was always sent for when trouble or illness came
to the household of a friend. She was not learned
or very accomplished. Her representation of The
Flood in cross-stitch worsted work, now hanging
over the chamber mantelpiece, began and ended her
achievements with the needle. She could sit down
to the piano in the twilight and play pieces that gave
delight to listening ears, and as a housekeeper her
fame went far and wide. "She makes the best
pickles of any woman I ever ate," was the comment of a rival, who would *not* yield to Miss Penelope the palm for preserves of watermelon rind
carved to resemble Chinese ivories. She was generous to a fault, tender, forgiving. To carry to her
one's sorrows was like lying down when tired on an

old-time feather-bed. And she adored novels. Gay's
taste for romance was omnivorous, hardly anything
coming amiss to her, but Miss Penelope liked chiefly
those many-volumed works where the cast included a
traitor, a misunderstanding, two riven hearts, a dying
heroine, and a lover on horseback arriving in time
for the last sigh.

Aunt Finetta, on the contrary, was given to no
melting at imaginary woes. She was a stern, hawk-
eyed woman, utterly out of keeping with her fairy-
tale appellation ; and was many years older than her
sister, whom she regarded as in some respects on a
par with their orphan grandniece Gay. The only survivors of a large family born in this house, she, more
than her sister, belonged to the bygones that possessed it. The old gray-white stucco pile, built by
their Scotch grandfather soon after his arrival in
the Virginian colony, had always been hand in glove
with Virginian history. No room but kept its tradition of some personage renowned in the stirring days
before and after the American Revolution. The epoch
of Miss Finetta's first appearance at Belhaven routs
and parties had been before the ebb-tide of Belhaven's prosperity. Her people had led the van of entertainments to strangers and townsfolk. Now all were
gone — friends, parents, fortune. The house fairly
echoed with haunting whispers of the past. Nothing
remained but the old walls, the old furniture, some
old servants, a genteel competence, sister Penelope,
and Gay. By and by she would be carried out to
take her place in the family vault, already crowded,
under the cedars of the old town burial-ground.

Gay was not troubled by such thoughts. She only lamented the cutting off, long before her birth, of their right of way to the river, by a city street. Once the gentry who came to drink tea in Princess Royal street used to stroll down, between box walks and under bowers of jasmine, to see their own ships set sail for England. After that period came the bustle of growing commerce; but now the long wharf jutting into the river, and the dingy warehouses with the twinkling, broken panes of glass, had passed under a spell of silence and decay. Forlorn as was their present aspect, Gay loved to steal down and sit dangling her feet over the edge of the rotting docks, to dream and wonder why every exciting thing "had been." Born a sailor's child, she longed to repeople these hushed spaces with the seafaring folk that had kept Belhaven town astir. In early childhood she had fed her imagination on the stories of their memorable doings on the deep when they sailed richly laden barks into pirate-haunted waters. Among many tales, her favorite, perhaps, was that of the merchantman homeward bound from London in 1792, chased and captured by the French frigate *Insurgente*, her crew and captain carried to Nantes, drawn up in a line in the prison yard, and every other man picked out for Madame Guillotine — the survivors escaping over the prison wall by using their blankets cut into strips and knotted into a rope. Gay liked to think the returning heroes of that adventure had set foot in safety upon the crumbling boards through which she now caught glimpses of water lapping upon emerald-vested piles.

As she grew older, such dreams of the sea had faded
and her ambition took another turn. She wanted to
go out and shine in the great world. If her father, the
lieutenant, had lived, Gay felt sure that her talents
would have had wider scope. She was impatient of
the calm routine, the church-going, the housekeeping,
the traditions, the long, dull streets with their cobblestones set in grass, in which no inexplicable sound
was ever heard. Oh! for something that she did not
understand—could not account for! Oh! for some
break in this monotony of peace!

Then Gay passed into a softer phase. She began
to look oftener in the glass, to tie her rough locks
under a ribbon topknot, to speculate about love and
lovers. That her own suitor should be tall, with
night-black hair, a dome-like brow, and a hidden
sorrow, was all she absolutely exacted of fate—the
rest was immaterial. Failing a romance on her own
account, she took the deeper interest in Aunt Penelope's. Even the purple-faced Dr. Fountain offered
a loophole of escape from the uneventfulness of life
in old Belhaven.

· "You may take Peggy and the basket and go to
market for me, Gay," Aunt Penelope had remarked,
a little flurried. "You know what we need; and be
sure Hodges sends us the right cut of the sturgeon.
Dr. Fountain likes his sturgeon stuffed and baked."

Gay winced over the unsentimental sturgeon, but
obeyed. Nothing she loved better than market-day
and a little brief authority.

The clean streets around the market-place were

crowded with country wagons from which the horses
had been unhitched to feed at the back. Inside,
under the old brick arches, was delicious shadow.
Out in the open part of the square a picturesque
medley of booths for the sale of fruit and flowers
and vegetables was shaded by awnings from the
May sun. All the country-side seemed to have rendered tribute in May-flowers. Even the fish-stalls,
with their shining spoils of the Potomac, and the
prosaic butchers' stands, had each its nosegay of
fresh mock-orange, lilac, snowball and althea. The
cries of imprisoned ducks and chickens rose above
the soft chatter of the negro women, gay and emu-
lous to sell their wares. Everybody was at leisure to
be civil, and what elsewhere is the mosquito-note
of business here subsided into the drone of honey-
bees at harvest.

"If that is n't Major Daisy with old Vulcan!" exclaimed Miss Gay to her attendant.

"Major Daisy larfin' roun' de wrong side uv he
mouf to-day, I reckon," said Peggy, sapiently. "Law,
honey, he 'sarves it, he suttinly do, fur lettin' ole Miss
give him de mittin fur Miss Pen. Shua 's you live
dere 's to be a weddin' in de fambly, cos I done fotch
it in coffee groun's an' in de keards."

"A wedding! Oh, Aunt Peggy!" cried Gay.

"You jes wait, chile. 'Pears like husbands is a
long time a-comin' to our house, but—(Look heah,
you niggah! Ef you blocks up our way I 'll make a
mashed persimmon uv you, mighty quick.) Ef on'y
ole Miss don' go discommodatin' Providence by shet-
tin' de do' in dis heah one's face—"

IN THE OLD MARKET.

"But, Aunt Peggy," said Gay, who knew the terms upon which the termagant lived with her own meek little consort, Mars, "I thought you don't approve of marrying."

"Laws, chile, who said I do? (None o' them to-marteses o' yourn, Miss Johnson. I 'm s'prised at you fur offerin' 'em to my young miss.) Men is triflin', no 'count critters, honey; but I s'pose de good Lawd knowed wot he was arter when he 'lowed dat husbands was to be."

Gay, more affected than she chose to admit by Peggy's prophecy,—for the old woman enjoyed great renown as a fortune-teller,—felt quite a pang of sympathy for Major David when they came up with the little gentleman, who was purchasing some rather diminutive chops to put into the large basket the colored butler carried upon his arm.

"Good morning, Miss Gay. Hope I see you well, ma'am," he said, with a flourishing bow. "Caught the old bachelor buying his dinner, eh? Well, it 's like keeping house for a canary, so Vulcan thinks; but I 'm blessed if I know what to get when I 'm by myself. And how are the good ladies this morning? Was a little afraid Miss Pen would have a return of her earache after going out on the porch to see the new moon o' Saturday."

The earache! How unrefined! No word, no consciousness of the presence of the hated rival in the Berkeley house! Gay felt defrauded of a dramatic situation.

"You know we 've staying company," she said, with a little toss of the head. "A most agreeable and eminent divine. The Reverend Joshua Fountain, a friend, a very old friend, of my aunts."

"Fountain? You don't say so. Why, of course I know old Fountain. We were at school together; and the boys—because of a hearty appetite—you know boys will give nicknames—they called him 'Gobbling Josh.' Ha! ha! I remember one day at our table—but it don't do to tell tales out of school. Why, of course—Josh married Miss Molly Patton, of Anne Arundel. I remember seeing those two Patton sisters—Miss Molly was the little foxy one—at the Greenbrier White in—let me see—what year—"

But Gay, with great dignity, interrupted him. "Dr. Fountain has been a widower for at least a year," she said; "and I think my aunts will be expecting me, as we've got to go to Convention presently—so good morning, Major Garnett."

She blamed herself afterward for this severity. In books, the discarded suitor always veils his real feeling by an assumption of indifference. She even pardoned, and determined to forget, the odious suggestion of "Gobbling Josh," although it returned to her mind more than once at the dinner-table that day, when the family, reinforced by a new arrival, another reverend appetite, sat down to enjoy the sturgeon, together with other bountiful provision of Peggy's and Aunt Penelope's best culinary skill. Further to promote good fellowship, Aunt Finetta had invited in her next-door neighbors, the Misses Bassett, two dear little old ladies, whose establishment was ruled over by an Angora cat always spoken of as "He," and whose fear of burglars had

induced them to invest in a man's hat and stick
kept prominently in view in their front hall.

The social supremacy of the clergy in Belhaven has
long been a fact accepted with resignation by her
citizens of secular avocations. It used to be said
by the disaffected lawyers, bankers, doctors and mer-
chants of the place that their women would give first
chance to any theologue, even were he the downiest
youngster from the famous school of divinity hard
by the town; that for such were held in store the
brightest smiles, the softest arm-chairs, the most but-
tery of muffins. Without accepting this slander, we
may admit the discouragement to a young man who
had requested the object of his hopes to be at home
to him, at finding her alone with a seminarian, prac-
tising "Come, Ye Disconsolate," at the melodeon.
And we have heard of a Belhaven serenade received
with enthusiasm by the maiden beneath whose window the darkness was aroused with the tune of
"Mary to the Saviour's Tomb," performed as a
solo on the French horn!

The only real dissipation Belhaven ever indulged
in was a convention, and the week was very gay.
Tripping over the newly washed bricks of the sidewalk, in the wake of ministerial coats, were seen
ladies in neat morocco slippers, their white stockings crossed with black ribbons, their bonnets and
mantillas looking as if just come out of silver paper
and smelling of vanilla bean. They flocked to every
sitting of the delegates, and in the intervals exchanged tea-parties and "dinings," at which each
housewife in turn was expected to try some new

recipe. With their eyes devoutly fixed upon the ex-
pounding doctor in the pulpit, they would, during
the services, be often torn by pangs as to whether
Aunt Judy would know when to take that cake out
of the oven, or whether she might not get "per-
jinkety" and overspice the soup. This state of
things was hard upon the doctrine, but comfortable
for the divines.

Under such conditions Dr. Fountain, who had arrived in Belhaven wearing his bereavement upon his
sleeve for all to see, cheered up amazingly. His allusions to the loved and lost, his sniffs at tributes to
her worth, became less frequent. He waxed even
playful in his heavy way. He made visits among
his old acquaintances, drank tea and assumed Sir
Oracle in many homes, but was steadfast in returning early to enjoy the society of the house in Princess Royal street. The Misses Bassett, who from
their parlor window saw everything, declared that
coming back to the scenes of his young life had
made the doctor lose ten years of his age. He
walked buoyantly, exchanged his broad-brimmed
hat of black straw for a white one with a black
band, and preached a sermon so full of hope for
humanity and love for his fellow-men as to sound
like the twittering of swallows from a chimney-top.
When the Misses Bassett asked Miss Penelope if
she did not find this discourse "most refreshing,"
Aunt Pen assented beamingly; though in truth the
dear old lady had dozed off at "thirdly, my beloved
brethren," not to awake till the benediction. Major
Daisy, stalking up the aisle of the church after

everybody else was seated, with the gloves usually carried in his hat still resting upon his wig, heard the sermon also, and said afterward, with a quizzical smile, that "Josh was taking notice," he presumed. Dr. Fountain, who had come to spend a week, remained with the Berkeleys an entire fortnight, and afterward took up his abode at the Mansion House Hotel, near by. It was understood by his congregation that he was traveling for his health.

And now little nothings, betokening which way the wind blew, began to multiply. He asked Aunt Penelope to play for him "My favorite air, the melody of Thomas Moore entitled:

'Believe me if all those endearing young charms
 Which I gaze on so fondly to-day.'"

He brought in a big bunch of hundred-leaf roses purchased in the market-place, and, after hovering uncertainly around Miss Penelope awhile, presented them to Gay. He talked a great deal of his home, and his dear girls, and of the fine watermelon crops in his part of the country. He presented "Doddridge's Sermons" to Miss Berkeley; Pope's "Essay on Man" to Miss Penelope; and to Gay a blue and gold volume of "Selected Poems of the Affections," at which she laughed, and of which she did not read ten lines. But as the intentions of her future Uncle Joshua were good, she thanked him sweetly and redoubled her acts of hospitable kindness.

One night Peggy, accustomed to visit her Miss

Penelope for purposes of gossip after that lady had retired to bed, found her time for calling was miscalculated. Miss Penelope, in a voluminous white wrapper, starched and frilled, was still upon her knees engaged in devotions that Peggy from experience knew were likely to be protracted beyond the limit of her own waiting powers. Peggy, therefore, in a strained and melancholy voice, observed:

"Miss Pen 's sayin' her pra'rs, ain't she? I jes wish she knowed Miss Fanny Bassett 's sont in to ax fur de loan uv a quart uv to-morrer mornin's milk fur breakfas'."

"Let her have the milk," came in hollow tones from beneath Miss Penelope's night-coif; and then, to Peggy's disappointment, down went the head in devotion deeper than before. What was to be done? Peggy, well aware of the dear lady's terror of a mouse, was not long at a loss. Taking a ball of wool from Miss Penelope's knitting-basket, she let it shoot across the floor to bring up against her mistress's protruding foot. With a shriek and a bound Miss Penelope sprang into bed, not to stop shivering until safely tucked in — deceitful Peggy searching everywhere, but of course in vain, for the most deadly enemy of her maiden peace.

"Look for it, Peggy. Kill it! The little wretch touched me. Oh, I can smell him still!"

"Dey worn't never nut'in' like de giniwine Berkeley nose fur smellin' low-down smells," said Peggy, emitting a series of alarming sounds. "Dar now, chile, I see him run into dat crack behin' de bureau, an' he 'll be too scart to come back dis away to-night.

Miss Pen — ! Shua 's you bawn dat gentleman uv yourn ain't gwine away from here 'thout co'tin' somebody. He 's suttinly sot on marryin'."

"Nonsense, Peggy," said Miss Penelope.

"He is dat, shua! An' husbands ain't so plenty in dis house. Now, chile, I jes want to speak a word in season. Ole Miss ain't a gwyne to las' forever, an' when she go, who 's to take keer uv you 'n' Miss Gay?"

"The Lord will provide, Peggy."

"S'posin' he will, you 'd better hold on to your beau dis time, tight. He ain't so purty as some; but he 's stiddy an' conformable-like, an' he 's got chillen to keep company wid Miss Gay."

"O Peggy, I 've thought of all that," said poor Miss Penelope. "Don't you suppose sister Finetta has been at me every day? I 'm sure I never saw her so possessed to take anybody's part."

"But you likes him jes one little teenchy bit, honey?" coaxed Peggy, guiltily conscious of a present in her pocket of a gold dollar bestowed by Dr. Fountain for encouragement received, when she had encountered the good gentleman walking up and down between her rows of cabbages and, with the familiar wheedling of her race, had contrived to let him know that his presence in the house was not unacceptable to the lower powers.

"Wait till he asks me, Peggy," answered Miss Penelope, who, resolutely pulling the counterpane up to her chin, refused to say another word.

THE afternoon following this momentous interview Gay was in the garden tying up her clove-

6

pinks, which persisted in dropping their heavy, luscious heads to mother earth. While thus employed, a shadow fell across her sunshine, and, looking up, she beheld the tall, black-coated form and rubicund visage of their reverend visitor.

WHAT followed has never been circumstantially told. But the aunts who were in the shady chamber napping over their books were surprised and shocked at the sudden, impetuous entrance of Miss Gay, with a crimson face and an agitated manner.

"He's a horrid, old, conceited thing; and I hope never to lay eyes on him again," she cried, dashing a lapful of carnations down upon the floor.

"Gay, I am astonished," remarked both of the ladies in duet. "Pray, child, whom do you mean?"

"Dr. Fountain," cried Gay, too furious to cry. "He thought I was *in love with him!* He said I'd encouraged him to stay. And he said he'd wrestled in prayer about me till he'd determined to overlook my youth and take me to — be — his — *wife!*"

"My dear, you must be dreaming," said Aunt Penelope, gently. Aunt Finetta was too thunderstruck to speak.

"No, no, it's perfectly, hatefully true. I despise him, but I despise myself still more. When I only meant to be kind to him because — be — cause —" Here Gay stopped and choked.

"It's my duty to inquire into this affair," said Miss Berkeley, moving majestically toward the door.

"Oh, you need n't!" said Gay. "He's gone!

He 's raging! When he had the impudence to take
my fingers in his old flabby hand and squeeze them,
I just pinched him — pinched him *awfully*, and made
him let me go."

Miss Berkeley stopped, undecided, with her hand
upon the knob. Then turning to her sister, a pained
look of inquiry came upon her face.

" Penelope?" she said.

" We all have been mistaken, sister," was the quick
answer. "I was doing my best to please you; but—
I 'm afraid—I feel relieved."

Two years after these events Gay's heart's desire
was realized. There came into the still Belhaven
streets such a stir and marshaling of troops that
the town was born again to be the war-post of the
days of Washington. And when presently the boys
in gray who had been rallied from Belhaven's homes
marched out, the boys in blue marched in. Needless
to say that, drawn from its rusty scabbard, the sword
he had carried in Mexico was offered by Major Garnett to his Virginia. As colonel of a regiment of in-
fantry he served at the two battles of Manassas, and
for several campaigns was heard of wherever there
was fighting to be done. Then the eager, yearning
friends shut up in Belhaven, and meeting in secret to
pray for the armies of the South, learned that General Garnett had lost an arm and a leg in battle, and
was lying, not expected to survive, at a hospital in
Richmond. For the first time in her life Gay saw a
blue light of fixed determination burn in the placid
orbs of Aunt Penelope. Overcoming all obstacles,

and braving danger and distress, Miss Penelope Berkeley pushed through the lines and went to Richmond.

"Do you know me, David?" she asked, at the moment when it was believed his gallant soul was passing to its reward.

"Know you, Pen?" he answered. "Why, I must be in heaven."

"THERE is n't much of me left, ma'am," he remarked, in the course of a few weeks, to his devoted nurse; "but there 's a body to hold my heart, and a hand to put the ring upon your finger. Nothing should part us now, Pen. Come, say you 'll be Mistress Garnett."

"O David! As if I had n't loved you all my life," sighed Miss Penelope.

GENERAL and Mrs. Garnett went back, after a while, to live in the old house, whence Aunt Finetta had been gathered to her fathers. Gay's own romance came to her in due season, as I shall have presently to tell. But long before that was finally accomplished she had given to Major Daisy the enthusiastic homage of her heart. "Between Pen and Gay," the dear old boy used to say, "I 've more hands and feet and coddling than any one man, much less half a man, deserves."

THE Reverend Joshua espoused a widow with six children, three farms, and a temper locally renowned. Old Peggy died firmly believing that her incantations, if not her diplomacy, had secured a husband to the ancient house of Berkeley.

## III

## MONSIEUR ALCIBIADE

TRANSPARENTLY gentle despot, who might have been led by the finger-tip of the youngest member of his class, was M. Alcibiade de St. Pierre, the Belhaven dancing-master, who gave also lessons in his native tongue. Nature had endowed him with a stationary scowl, his mustaches curled wildly, and he bore upon the brow a cicatrix that caused his pupils to liken him to the swashbuckler heroes of Dumas, Scott, or Cervantes. In outward appearance he was Aramis, Athos, Porthos, and D'Artagnan in one, with a dash of Le Balafré and Don Quixote thrown in.

Although this picturesque personage was a comparative new-comer in the town, the forebear of M. Alcibiade had arrived in America as pendant to an expedition supplying an interesting chapter of frontier history. Early in the spring of 1790 came into port at Belhaven a party of French immigrants en-

gaged by Playfair, an English agent, and De Sois-
sons, a nimble-tongued deceiver of his compatriots,
in behalf of an enterprise organized in New England,
and styled the Ohio Land Company, to people the wilderness near the Kanawha River, beyond the western woods of Virginia. Among the travelers, whose
weary hearts beat high with hope as they touched
the shore of a fancied El Dorado, were men skilled
in the exquisite handicrafts of a perfected civiliza-
tion. Carvers there were of furniture like wooden
lacework; beaters of fine brass fashioned into *rocaille*
decorations; painters of shepherds piping to their
fair, of Cupids turning somersaults in chains of
roses; harpsichord-tuners; makers of gilded carriages; varnishers of panels that shone like mirrors;
disciples of Boule and Martin; confectioners; perru-
quiers—and all, by a fine irony of fate, bound for a
log-hut settlement, where the cry of savage beasts, or
the war-whoop of the deadly Indian, was to be their
nightly lullaby.

What eloquence had prevailed upon these hapless beings to believe they were to be the founders
of a brave new Paris in the western hemisphere,
their wily managers alone could tell. The first in-
stalment of the five hundred Frenchmen said to
have been thus deluded, numbering with their wives
and children about sixty, after much waiting at
Belhaven, their souls within them vexed by home-
sickness and hope deferred, split up into variously
minded factions. Some pressed on, under charge
of a long-delayed messenger of the company, to the
frontier; others put their all into a return passage

to France; and a few elected to remain and try
their fortunes in the little town, which in those
days had no end of ambitious projects for future
greatness.

One of these prudent ones was a gay old bachelor,
M. Alcibiade St. Pierre, self-styled "Hair-Dresser to
the Court of France." He opened a snug little shop,
where the gentry of town and country dropped in to
have their perukes dressed and tied, to be shorn, per-
fumed and shampooed, after the latest fashions in
vogue before Alcibiade had set sail for the New
World. He was sometimes sent for to bleed, or to
apply leeches, and his *mille-fleurs* graces impressed
the townspeople mightily. As his trade increased,
Alcibiade was called on to lament the sad fortunes
of his fellow-immigrants. Most of those who became
frontiersmen had succumbed to want and hardships,
had met the horrors of Indian massacre, or had
gone under in the collapse of an international speculation that carried down its promoters in the crash.
From those who returned to France had come dol-
orous accounts of commotion in their beloved capital.
Decidedly, thought M. Alcibiade, it were better to
stagnate in Belhaven than be forced by a mob in
Paris to dress the head of some former patron upon
a pike!

Simple-minded, kindly, cheery as *le petit homme
gris*, the little hair-dresser became a great favorite.
A trig Scotch lassie, daughter of a settler, having
fallen in love with him, the father consented to the
match on the condition that the intended son-in-law
would renounce his French patronymic and trans-

late himself into plain "A. Peters" upon his sign and in his official signature. And thus it came to pass that, instead of the stylish frontispiece so flattering to town pride, there arose above the shop door an announcement remaining there until its blue and gold were dimmed by time:

A. PETERS, LADIES' AND GENTS' HAIR-
DRESSER AND BARBER.

And, farther down:

WIGS AND TOUPETS.
DISEASES OF THE SCALP.
ONGUENTS AND SCENTS.
HAIR-POWDER, ROUGE AND PATCHES.
ATTENDANCE AT HOUSE FOR BALLS AND
ROUTS.

Also:

TEETH PULLED, AND LIVELY LEECHES
CONSTANTLY IN STOCK.

By the smiles and blushes of his buxom bride the gallant Alcibiade considered himself well paid for his self-sacrifice. Continuing to prosper, he gave hostages to hair-dressing in the shape of several little lads who spoke English with a broad

Scotch burr, French not at all, and, later in life,
seized with nostalgia, emigrated with his family to
end his days on the soil that gave him birth.

Old Mr. Peters had become a figment of tradition in the town when his grandson, the present
Alcibiade, appeared upon the scene. To the ances-
tral St. Pierre the new representative had prefixed
a patrician "de," vaguely explained as having been
resumed by the family on recovering possession of
estates lost in the French Revolution. To plain
people in Belhaven this prefix was interpreted to
be an initial letter D, doing duty for a middle
name not given. As for the estates, they must
have been limited to the amount aptly if not
elegantly designated by the French Commandant
Marin in the conference with the Half-King of the
Six Nations, recorded by Washington in 1753, when
he said, "Child, you talk foolish; there is not so
much land as the black of my nail yours."

When first arrived in Belhaven, the poor Frenchman was indeed in a pitiable plight. The attention
of the town was called to him by certain readings
and recitations in his own language, advertised to
be given in Lafayette Hall.

Gay Berkeley, who, with her maiden aunt Penelope, had gone into Mrs. Dibble's shop to purchase
pens and writing-paper, picked up from the counter
a long sheet of manuscript that excited her amused
curiosity. It was apparently a programme, written on foolscap in a fine copper-plate hand, and ex-
pressed in a queer French-English that would have
been a credit to the manual known to fame as the

"Portuguese Grammar and Guide to Polite Conversation."

On my arrival from the France, me Alcibiade de St. Pierre, Chevalier of the Legion of Honor and ex-artist of the theatres of Paris, do make hurry to throw myself at the feet of illustrious citizens of Belhaven, with a presentment special of selections from the immortal Racine et Corneille, such presentment to have place Hall Lafayette, the Monday evening to follow. Receive, ladies and gentlemen, my distinguished homages and impressed salutations your very humble serviteur.

"What in the world is this, Mrs. Dibble?" asked the young lady, with dimpling cheeks.

"Indeed, Miss Gay, I told the Chevalier that it would n't be long catchin' the eye o' my best customers," responded Mrs. Dibble, complacently. "I helped him out a bit with the words he did n't know. Dear heart, if it was n't only but for the handwritin', as good as Mr. Johnson's nephew that was put in State's prison for forgery, pore fellow, he that used to practise here with fine nibs an' broad nibs, writin' cards — spread eagles with your name in curlicues comin' out o' their beaks — an' true-lovers' knots an' doves, if 't was a new-married pair. Miss Penelope, I 'm ashamed to say I 'm clean out o' quills; but old Farmer Berry up at the cross-roads, the only one I can trust to pick the geese properly, 'll bring me a new lot to-morrow. Miss Gay, now, she 's new school, 'n uses steel — sand, ma'am? Yes; of course. The usual quantity? Here 's sweet note-paper, Miss Gay, just received from Baltimore, the tip o' the mode, they say —

pale pink an' skim-milk blue. Plain white, did you
say, miss? Yes; I 've some cream-laid, like you 've
always used befo'. If you 've nothin' better to do,
ladies, 't would be a charity to that pore Mounseer
to patronize his performance a Monday night. If
't was only for old times' sake, Miss Penelope,
ma'am; many 's the head he 's dressed — I mean
his grandfather 's dressed — for your fam'ly. Yes;
old Mr. Peters's grandson, as I 'm alive, ma'am, an'
the entertainment most genteel. Selections from
Corneel an' Raycine; fifty cents for adults, twenty-
five for children, an' a special reduction for ladies'
schools. I thought there 'd be a chance to get the
young gentlemen from Mr. Penhallow's Academy;
but the Chevalier kinder shriveled up at the men-
tion o' boys, an' said 't was too hard to keep up the
true dignity o' the drama when they was present —
Lord knows, since I took to keepin' sweet stuff in
t' other winder I 'm up to the ways o' boys. If
it 's only a penny horse-cake — comin' back as bold
as brass, with the hind legs cat off, declarin' they 's
found a dead fly instead of a currant for the eye,
an' wantin' their money or another cake —"

"Do take some tickets, Aunt Pen," pleaded Gay.

"You know my sister does not approve of anything theatrical, my love," whispered Aunt Penelope. "Most of our church-members think with
her. To be sure dear mama used often to tell us
of the time when General Washington and his lady,
and Miss and Master Custis, drove up to stop two
nights at grandpapa's, expressly to attend 'The Tragedy of Douglas,' by Mr. Home, and a play called

'The Inconstant; or, The Way to Win Him.' Mama saw all the entertainments of the kind, I believe. It was thought of differently in those days."

"Doctor Falconer," ventured Gay, mentioning an eminent divine, "quoted, when he last drank tea with us, a passage from Racine. And these are only recitations, auntie, no acting or costumes."

"Oh, in that case," said Aunt Penelope, taking out her purse, "you may give me four tickets, Mrs. Dibble, and you may invite two members of your French class, child. Seats in the second row, if you please, Mrs. Dibble. In a thing of this kind it is well to be near enough to study the expression of the performer's face; and one likes to forget the crowd when it 's poetry. I 'm sure sister Finetta will be pleased to hear about old Mr. Peters's grandson."

Lafayette Hall was a dingy, ill-lighted room over the second floor of the building in which Mrs. Dibble kept her shop. To the young people it was associated with the intermittent delights of performances by trained dogs and canaries; by Blind Tom, a negro pianist who could repeat every air suggested to him by the audience, and play better with his hands behind him than most of his hearers in the natural attitude; by the tuneful Hutchinson family, who stood in a row and warbled; by jugglers always interesting, and returned missionaries, less alluring to the young; of May exhibitions of female seminaries, whereat the pupils in book-muslin with arbor-vitæ wreaths recited before applauding parents poems in honor of their queen, and were afterward regaled with lemonade and cake. It was there that Gay, as first lady-in-waiting, had once retired behind the queen's throne in tears, because her majesty had not scrupled to twit her with wearing one of Aunt Pen's muslins "made over"— which was too true.

Even now Gay could not divest herself of the exhilaration produced by the sight of that green baize curtain and the oil-lamps serving as foot-lights. When, on the evening of the Chevalier's *début*, she came into the hall, she nodded on every side to her friends, with a feeling that this was life. Mrs. Dibble, whose person was attired in grass-green *mousseline de laine*, with a wide collar of dotted net, trimmed with cotton lace, took tickets at the door; and in a conspicuously good seat sat Viney Piper, the little day-dressmaker, whose passion for the drama led her to patronize every respectable show that came to town. Viney had arrived upon the opening of the doors at six o'clock, and the performance was advertised to begin at half-past seven. She was an odd-looking, albino sort of creature, with pinkish eyes and eyelids, pale flaxen hair, and a hook-nose much to one side of her face. The Chevalier, entering the hall, had caught sight of her on his way to the rear of the stage, and forthwith executed a sweeping bow that Viney thought the perfection of foreign elegance.

When the hall was fairly filled, and the shuffling of feet announced the right degree of impatience on the part of the audience, the curtain, pulled up by the performer himself, rose upon a stage empty

7

save for a small pine table displaying a white china water-pitcher and a goblet. M. Alcibiade, wearing a suit of rusty black, with a scarlet satin stock and white kid gloves, an order in his button-hole, his hair fiercely ruffled, and his eyes gleaming at some foe unknown, holding a dinner-knife in his clenched hand, stalked on the scene. At this alarming apparition a little girl sitting by her mama burst into tears, and had to be consoled with gum-drops from the parental pocket, interspersed with audible assurances that the gentleman meant no harm. Opening his lips, Alcibiade poured forth a cataract of words, of which the most advanced French scholars in Miss Meechin's senior class could make neither head nor tail. He raved, he roared, he ranted; then, seizing a goblet from the table, he half filled it with water, and, holding the dagger in his other hand, advanced to the footlights calling on Heaven to end his woes. At last, drinking the contents of the poisoned cup, he threw away the dinner-knife, and fell with a gurgling groan and a crash that made the lamps rattle in the chandelier. This, by agreement with Mrs. Dibble, was the signal for that worthy lady to hurry behind the scenes and let fall the curtain on the direful sight; but she, unfortunately, stood like a stock, averring afterward that her blood was that cruddled with awr she could n't 'a' budged a mite! Next, M. Alcibiade, coming slowly back to life, sat up to confront the audience with a smile of absolute fatuity, then, scrambling to his feet, bowed, kissed his hand, and, going off, let the green baize descend on act the first.

It was long since Belhaven had enjoyed such a merry spectacle. The school-girls leading off with infectious giggles, every bench caught the contagion, and only Viney Piper, mopping real tears from her eyes, announced herself a connoisseur of true art.

The rest of the programme, although less explosive, met with hysterically suppressed mirth. Before its close, indeed, the audience had filtered slowly from the hall, leaving only the faithful Viney and Mrs. Dibble, the newspaper-carrier (who was stone-deaf), a scrub-woman with her baby in arms, and a few citizens who exacted their money's worth.

It was evident that provincial taste had not been educated to the dramatic standard of old Mr. Peters's grandson. Alcibiade, failing in other occupations, sank from poverty to want. One day when Miss Viney Piper, arriving at the Berkeley house in Princess Royal street, had established herself in the sewing-room, the ladies in submissive attitudes before her, the little dressmaker could hardly wait to dispose of business before introducing the subject near her heart.

"Just keep on running up them skirt-widths, Miss Gay; an' Miss Penelope, ma'am, you could be goffer-in' that sleeve while I get the body ready to try on," she said, marshaling her forces like a general in command. "Did you hear the news — that old Mr. Peters's grandson ain't expected to live the day out? Fairly starved, I reckon, 'fore he 'd let Mrs. Dibble know, an' he sleepin' in a hole of an attic at the Drovers' Hotel — kinder low fever, nothin' catchin', the doctor says, but nothin' to bring him up again.

Such a beautiful genius he is, ma'am, an' a temper like a child, for all he looks so fierce."

"Starving! What do you mean, Viney?" said Miss Penelope, excitedly. "Go, Gay, fetch me my bonnet and mantilla, and help Susan to pack a basket with some things. How comes it that nobody knew?"

"It 's all right for the present, Miss Penelope, ma'am," said Viney, blushing. "That 's what 's kep' me a little late this mornin'. I took up a few trifles, an' Mrs. Dibble she 's got somebody to mind the store, and is to stay with him all day. But if you 'd let Peggy put on a chicken to boil down for jelly, it would n't be wasted, even if —" here she swallowed once or twice and stabbed her pincushion — "if the pore Mounseer can't make no use of it."

The "pore Mounseer," however, surviving the day under Mrs. Dibble's kindly care, and finding no lack of nourishment during the days that followed, was, with the assistance of a subscription among some charitable people, transferred in the course of a week to a spare room let to single gentlemen by Mrs. Piper, Viney's mother, which by happy accident had been recently vacated.

The Pipers lived in one of the small frame-houses built to open directly upon the moss-encircled bricks set diagonally in the ancient sidewalk of a modest street. The door-stone of white marble was accounted in the neighborhood a badge of distinguishing elegance, as was also a small brass oval serving as a bell-pull, when most people used knockers, or "knuckles," the gossips would aver. The late Mr.

Piper had been a seafaring man, and had risen to be first mate of the brig *Polly and Nancy*, when, on a return voyage from Cadiz with a cargo of fruit, salt, and wines bound for Belhaven port, he was swept overboard in a hurricane and lost.

The best room of the little house into which one stepped out of the street direct, was a sort of marine museum like a chill grotto, suggesting a mermaid's clutch or the grip of shark's teeth. Here Mrs. Piper did not care to raise the shades, except at one side window permanently darkened by a trellis overgrown with a vine of the Isabella grape. The children of Miss Viney's customers liked to be sent to make appointments with that busy little body; for Mrs. Piper, too deaf to answer questions, and droning her explanations in a sing-song voice, always showed them around the museum with great affability. The old woman usually sat in a clean kitchen opening upon the back yard, where, under the damson-trees and amid the hundred-leaf rosebushes, were constructed little winding walks, edged with shells, and leading up to seats made of a whale's backbone.

After the Chevalier de St. Pierre had succeeded in obtaining classes in dancing and deportment that enabled him to live, and had settled down to become a fixture in the widow's house, his spare moments were given to cultivating flowers in the beds between the shell-bordered walks. Everything grows easily in soft Belhaven air, and soon the Pipers' garden became a proverb in the place. Mrs. Piper's only complaint against her lodger was couched in the expressive phrase, "The Lord knows how often he empties his water-jug"; but even a distaste for ablution yielded in time to the insistent cleanliness of his surroundings. Sometimes, to cheer "Madame Pipère" in her solitude, Alcibiade would descend to the kitchen and proffer to the old woman, knitting in her sunny window-seat, "a leetle divertissement from ze classique drama of La France." He had a *vrai* inspiration for the stage, St. Pierre confessed to Viney, and but for political intrigue would be now in his rightful place on the boards of the Théâtre Français. These exhibitions, repeating the celebrated performance of his début at Lafayette Hall, were as deeply and religiously admired by the widow as by her daughter.

One day occurred a variant upon the usual exercise. Alcibiade had always treated poor lank Viney as if she were one of the great ladies of the court in bondage to his ancestor's curling-tongs; but she was unprepared for the scene that greeted her return when, having stepped down to Slater's for a spool of "forty" cotton, she found the Chevalier in his best black suit, wearing white kid gloves, and holding a bouquet in one hand, kneeling at Mrs. Piper's feet and kissing her finger-tips with reverence.

"I ask you, madame, for the hand of your beautiful and admirable child in marriage," was what Viney and the whole neighborhood within ear-shot heard him roar.

Viney, with all her good qualities, was a bit of a virago. The absurdity of the proceeding, and the sense that her adjacent acquaintances were laughing

at her affairs, flooded her thin skin with blushes, and
her soul with anger. While Mrs. Piper, scared out
of her wits, was about to open her lips for a feeble
screech, Viney whisked into the kitchen, snatched
Alcibiade's bouquet, threw it away into a parsley-
bed, and boxed the professor's ears.

"You 'd better believe I give 'im a piece of my
mind," she narrated afterward to Miss Penelope and
Gay. "But, bless you, he cried so pitiful, an' begged
our pardons so kind o' honorable, I had not the heart
to turn him out o' the house like I threatened to.
Them white kids, Miss Gay! An' at his age, an'
mine! The notion 's too cryin' ridic'lous." And she
snapped a seam into the beak of her sewing-bird with
vicious emphasis, giving at the same time a sidelong
glance into the mirror, and a complacent toss of the
head.

No one could be long in the Chevalier's company
without discovering that a very dove of gentleness
and affectionate gratitude dwelt in his gaunt envelop
of flesh. So, restraining his pretensions as a lover,
he meekly accepted Miss Viney's fiat, and went about
the town looking as warlike as ever, but inwardly
carrying a broken spirit. One of his dancing-class encountered him crossing a windy common in the sub-
urbs of the town pursued by a flock of geese, from
whose sibilant obloquy he was making nervous efforts to escape; and it was known to the boys and
girls that the Chevalier was always alarmed by the
apparition of a spider or a cow. No wonder the
young people decided that Alcibiade had been reduced to pulp by Miss Viney's vigorous rejection of

his suit. The little dressmaker's peppery temper was familiar to the offspring of her customers, from whom she would stand no trifling around her temporary throne in their respective households.

When the war between the States broke out, Viney seemed to have found her destined vocation as a red-hot secessionist. Not very clear, fundamentally, as to what she resented on the part of the national authorities at the other end of the Long Bridge, some eight miles away, she threw out her rebel banner on the wall, sang "Dixie" in her shrill treble, declaimed, protested, and, in short, kept everybody in her vicinity in a boiling state of excitement about the condition of political affairs. When the Belhaven regiments went on to Richmond or Manassas, Viney stitched her fingers to the bone making shirts for them, while Mrs. Piper knit socks of gray wool as fast as her needles could fly. They also turned out a number of the white linen havelocks and gaiters adopted by one of the companies and afterward discarded as a too shining mark for opposing riflemen. Viney trotted to the train to see the boys go off, and stood there in the crowd, cheering and waving with the best. As she watched the last car recede on two gleaming lines of iron, its rear platform thronged with gesticulating shapes in gray, she felt her heart inflate and her stature grow with a yearning desire to go out and fight, or do something helpful in their ranks.

When she turned to walk home that afternoon of balmy spring, there, haunting her footsteps, was the faithful Alcibiade. He looked into her watery blue eyes as if imploring to be allowed to speak his sympathy.

"Have it out, an' be done with it, for gracious sake," said Viney, pettishly. His smooth-finished black coat, his waxed mustache, the bunch of jonquils in his buttonhole, fretted her beyond endurance.

"Those tears for the brave they are a benison," said Alcibiade, sentimentally. "Who would not be inspired by them to deeds of glory?"

"It 's not the boys I 'm cryin' for," said Viney. "It 's us that are left behind and have got to put our necks under the vandal's heel." That "vandal" afforded a famous outlet for secession wrath in those days; it may be doubted whether the war could have been carried on without him. "Oh! if 't worn't for mother, d' ye think I 'd stay? I 'd go to-morrow, an' carry a water-pail to fill canteens; or I 'd nurse in hospitals—or anything."

"It is a noble, a sacred cause," replied the Chevalier, looking down at the toe of his varnished boot to avoid the needle-point of her eye. "You will permit me, chère Mees Viney, to mingle with yours my prayers for its success? When I think that this Virginia that has sheltered two exiles of our house — my ancestor, who came here to find a home, a bride, a thousand friends, a thousand tendernesses; and me, less fortunate, but ever grateful for the hour that brought you, an angel of goodness, to my rescue in distress—"

"That 's neither here nor there," interrupted Viney, cruelly. "Besides, it was as much Mrs. Dibble as me, anyway."

"But you will not deny me the privilege of sharing your patriotic anxiety for the welfare of the troops? You will allow my heart to beat in unison with yours?"

"Nobody ain't a-preventin' your heart doin' what it pleases," said the uncompromising lady of his love, now fairly out of patience with his phrasing. "But it's deeds, not words, that show what a man's worth nowadays. When I think what a fool I used to be 'bout fine talkin', an' how I believed if a feller spread himself in speechifyin' he was boun' to be a hero, it makes me fairly sick. I'd rather have the little finger o' one o' them privates that's in the train we hear whistlin' up yonder — bless their souls! — than the whole body of a dandy Jim that stays at home. But, law me! I'm foolish talkin' such stuff to *you*."

Foolish and manifestly unjust, we will agree with her; but Viney's seed was not sown upon barren soil, as we shall see. From that date the Chevalier's mustaches lost their jaunty curl, his eye its martial fire. The dancing-school declining with the growth of military rule in town, his occupation was chiefly to walk along the streets picking up such rumors and crumbs of gossip about the movements of either army as might bring a spark of interest into the orbs of Miss Viney on his return to the widow's house.

The days of June wore on, and Viney's temper, taxed by anxiety about the issue of the approaching battle, became more tart, her taunts more frequent; but the Chevalier suddenly seemed to take heart and to walk with a firmer tread. One night

he did not return to sleep in his tidy bedroom, and
Viney, going into it, found a letter addressed to
herself upon the table.

Adieu, my benefactress, beautiful inspiration of my unworthy
life [the Chevalier had written], I fly to win the approval of
your noble tears or to sleep eternally upon the soldier's bloody
couch.   To you, in this supreme moment, I dare avow a truth
for which my manhood does not blush — that I have, until now,
held back because of a weakness of temperament that made
my soul blanch at thought of the soldier's baptism of fire.
Now that the struggle is over, I am resolved to ally myself with
the armies of the South that has given me a shelter, and given
me you, adored one, whose hand I embrace in spirit, with that
of your respected mother; to whom, and to you, the salutations
the most distinguished of your all-devoted     ALCIBIADE.

"The land o' Dixie!" cried out Miss Viney.   "If
that pore creeter's in earnest, I'll never draw a free
breath till he gets back."

M. Alcibiade was very much in earnest.   A few
days later Miss Viney had a visit from a lawyer
who informed her that the Frenchman, before going through the lines to enlist in the Southern
army, had caused to be drawn up a will bequeath-
ing to her some hundreds of dollars which by fru-
gality and care he had saved during his residence
beneath their roof.   Viney had an honest crying-
fit after the lawyer left, and, putting on her bonnet, sped down to Princess Royal street to take
counsel with the Misses Berkeley as to the best
way of tracing the absent one and conveying to
him some token of her appreciation and regard.
Those ladies could give her little hope.   They prom-

ised, however, to write recommending Alcibiade to
the care and kind offices of their friends in Belhaven regiments, should the Frenchman find his
way among his old acquaintances and pupils; and
with this Viney was forced to be content.

After Bull Run, Manassas; and after Manassas,
a breathing-space in which North and South held
themselves in check, dreading to pierce the veil
shadowing the future of the conflict. In the dusk
of a warm summer evening, when Viney had carried out a bucket of fresh water with which to
drench and cool the already clean bit of pavement
appertaining to their front door, a country wagon
with a hooded canopy of canvas, drawn by mules
and driven by a long-legged rustic in a linen duster,
wearing a broad straw hat, pulled up beside the curb.
Inside was heard the cackle of resentful fowls. The
driver, carrying a basket of eggs, leaned over and
accosted her:

"No; I don't want anything to-day, I'm 'bliged to
ye," began Viney — and broke down with a gasp.
"Good Lord! It's you, Mounseer?"

"It is, charming Mees Viney," said the pretended
farmer, with a warm grasp of her hand. "Hush!
Not a word that the neighbors can overhear."

"But I don't understand; you are not in the army,
after all?"

"There are ways and ways of being a soldier," he
went on in a low whisper. "Believe me when I tell
you I have kept my word. Take a few of these eggs
and count them into a dish or basket — yes, your
apron will do — that I may go on talking without

fear. Then I will find it troublesome to gif you change."

"But where in the land did you come from?" she asked, burning with curiosity.

"*Ma foi*, from a Union camp to-day, where the soldiers have left me little to sell to you, *belle dame*. To-morrow at daybreak — for I shall find fresh mules outside the town — I present myself to a general whom a Frenchman is proud to serve — ze peerless Beauregard."

"You are — you are — a sp —" she began, her face blanched, her teeth chattering.

"Never mind what I am; let me but look once more upon that face of which I so often dream, and then I must hasten away."

"Oh, go, go!" she pleaded. "It was perfect madness for you to come here. Not ten minutes ago a patrol of Yankee soldiers walked down this street."

"Bah!" he said, with a shrug, "have I not enjoyed the company of their compatriots all day? But for your sake I will go. Have no fear, *belle* Viney; you will hear from me again."

Was this the timid, the cringing Alcibiade? Viney asked herself all through a sleepless night. Many and many a night thereafter she was destined to toss and wonder as to his fate. In the autumn she had a line from him, left by a wood-seller from far up in the interior of the county; he was safe and well, and still in the service of the employer who retained him when he had seen her last; and he was always her devoted and faithful A. de St. P.

8

After that a blank of long years extending to the close of the dreadful war.

Viney had given him up for dead, of course; had put on mourning and made her mother do the same; and everybody said how strange it was that Viney Piper should make all that fuss about a man that just walked out of her house one day and gave her the "go-by" without a word. She could never persuade herself to touch a penny of his bequest; but had consulted her confidante, Miss Penelope, about the propriety of using it for a fine monument to be erected to his memory in the Belhaven graveyard, when the correspondent of a New York paper, mousing around the old Virginian town for material, announced to the public that he had discovered the identity of the famous and daring rebel scout, Peters, who, after countless adventures, and escaping the noose a dozen times by a miracle, had disappeared from sight. This dashing character, it was confidently stated, was none other than a so-called French dancing-master, known at the time as St. Pierre, who had lived in Belhaven pursuing his harmless occupation for some years prior to the war.

In the comments of the press upon this announcement more than one reminiscence of Peters was soon given currency; and presently the editor of a journal in an obscure western town wrote to the New York paper that Peters, *alias* St. Pierre, *alias* no-one-knew-what beside, was then actually residing in the family of a charitable Frenchman of his locality, having survived a wound and an imprisonment that had left him helpless upon his benefactor's hands.

When this was published Viney's friends saw the little woman smile. Then she cried, then she fell down on her knees and thanked God for his mercy, and lastly she packed her little trunk and set off for Illinois.

"You have come to me, and I was too proud to bring the remains of me to you, *belle* Viney!" said Alcibiade, when she arrived. "It is enough for me to see you, to forget that dungeon where I laid so long."

Poor little, homely Viney was utterly overcome. She took his thin hand, with the claw-like fingers, and, stooping down, kissed it and cried over it.

"Lord, lay not this sin to my door!" she said, gazing on the wreck before her with a sudden, bitter self-reproach. "O Mounseer, tell me that you forgive me for what I drove you to, for I'll never forgive myself."

"Listen to me, Mees Viney," the Frenchman said, looking about him anxiously to see that no one overheard. "You have done for me what a thousand times, in peril of my neck, in cold, in hunger, in a prison cell, I have thanked you for—you have made of me a man! *Bon Dieu*, a man!"

VINEY brought him back to the little chamber beneath the roof of Mrs. Piper's house, where the two women nursed him into comparative comfort; health he might never fully know again. In summer-time, his chair rolled out upon one of the shell-bordered walks, he would remain gazing in absolute content upon Viney sitting on the door-step with her work.

In his eyes she was always beautiful; and when, with many misgivings, she one day consented to let Dr. Falconer, with Aunt Penelope and Gay as witnesses, step into the grotto of marine curiosities and make her Madame Alcibiade, the ex-spy straightened up with something of his old dancing-master's grace.

"*Tiens!* I have won the flower of womanhood," he said. And so he thought to the last.

## IV

## GAY'S ROMANCE

### I

WHEN Gay Berkeley, a bright-eyed girl in quaint made-over frocks, took her walks abroad with Great-Aunt Penelope, who was arrayed in a large bonnet with tulle ear-tabs and a shawl of China crape trailing limp over a black silk gown, she used to think there could be no spot on earth in which so many interesting things had happened, and so many interesting people had lived, as in old Belhaven. Every house, street, paving-stone, evoked from the maiden aunt's unfailing repertoire a reminiscence. When Miss Pen met on the sidewalk some other large-bonneted lady, they talked together of mysterious has beens; and, before they parted, the lady would generally take the girl's chin in hand to look her in the face, and tell Gay that she was the image of her great-grandmother, or that she had her Uncle Marmaduke's own nose.

Gay, who in those days looked at most things from a Castle of Otranto standpoint, liked the externals of her birthplace, where, early left an orphan, she had always dwelt under the care of her father's aunts. She could appreciate the picturesque value of its grass-grown thoroughfares, bordered with blocks of houses, mostly of red brick faced with white, many of them detached and set comfortably back in brick-walled gardens harboring the sun; its venerable churches, inns, lodges, market-places, remaining there to tell of the great founders of the town; its wide area of surrounding landscape, to which, from an eminence beyond the city limits, visiting strangers were proudly introduced. From Shooter's Hill, looking across the caterpillar structure of the Long Bridge, one saw the white gleam of the Capitol dominating the roofs and spires of Washington; the colonnades of Arlington House; the beautiful, broad Potomac as far as Gunston, Mount Vernon, and Belvoir; the lovely valley of Cameron — all these enframed in undulating woods. Whenever Gay heard travelers dilate upon the Rhine, the Tweed and the Thames, she was conscious of a bridling desire to bid them view the Potomac from the top of Shooter's Hill, and die.

But this much any one could see, and still can see. More important in coloring her ideas was the daily intercourse with a community of people who belonged to the semi-feudal and essentially aristocratic side of early American society, even then gliding away like the sands of an hour-glass. Everybody they knew had somewhere touched history; everybody kept tra-

ditions rubbed up with chamois leather and set side-
wise on shelves. Life flowed so tranquilly. The
visits, tea-drinkings, church-goings, benevolent soci-
eties, never developed anything newer than the re-
current tragedies of birth and death. Young men
who grew up there stretched their limbs, inflated
their chests, looked away over at the far horizon,
and left the town. Everything in the way of stir or
bustle was executed with such genteel deliberation
that, like the immortal Joe in Pickwick, it fell asleep
*in itinere.*

But to a speculative young person like Miss Gay
there was entertainment to be found, and she well
knew where to look for it. When not poring over
the old books in the Princess Royal street house
where she was born, Gay studied human nature in
the homes of her aunts friends. By Miss Penelope,
who was a mine of genealogical information, she was
continually fed with stories ; and, when in search of
the concrete forms of excitement, what better than
to perch on the edge of the kitchen table where black
Peggy was rolling out her dough, and to elicit the
marvels that the old cook, "when i' the vein," would
pour out in accents as rich and soft as oil?

The drawback to Peggy's narratives was her anxiety to assert herself as an eye-witness of all events.
In the matter of Washingtoniana, especially, the old
woman, accustomed to be questioned by strangers as
to the minutest recollections cherished by the town
of its most illustrious hero, was very tenacious of
associating herself in every scene described.

"Think of it, Aunt Peggy," Gay said once, when

on a visit to the kitchen, "Auntie has been telling me that her grandfather had just finished building this house when George Washington was recruiting his ragged volunteers to march against the French on the Ohio. She says her grandpapa told her the young lieutenant-colonel was a long-legged, gawky fellow, with big hands, and so solemn the Belhaven girls would run away from him whenever he came near. But they sang a different tune when he came back from the wars."

"Wot you tellin' me, chile?" quoth Peggy, contemptuously. "Think I ain't heard Miss Lucindy beg Miss Sally many a time to go down in de parlor an' 'ceive Kunnel Wash'n'ton, 'stid uv her? An' Miss Sally say as how she would n' do no sich a thing 'less Miss Lucindy promise to let her wear dat blue padu'-soy uv her'n next Sunday to Christ Church. An' all de while dem gals was a-'sputin', dat poor young feller was a-coolin' his heels in de werry place whar' ole Miss got her big arm-cheer in dis day."

"Why, Aunt Peggy," exclaimed Gay, "that was in 1754!"

"Who said it worn't?" queried the old woman, testily.

"It would make you—oh! at least a hundred and twelve years old—"

"How 's I gwine to git my dinnah, like to know?" interrupted Peggy. "Reckon Miss Pen 'll come out cheer an' riz Richa'd Henry roun' my years nex' thing. You Cynthy! Hurry an' put dat crock on ice, ef you 'spec' to git de bonnyclabber sot fur tea! Mars! Awe, Mars! Nem o' Gawd, niggah, think fire burn 'dout wood? Hain't heerd yo' ax strike a lick sence you chop my chickens' hades off. You Trip! String dem snaps 'fo' I bust yo' cocoanut."

In the sudden whirlwind Gay and her questions vanished from the scene.

No story of the past hidden behind Belhaven house-fronts had quite such power to charm Gay's imagination as that of two stricken sisters who lived at a place called the Poplars, just outside the town, their sole companion a slave-woman, as gray and as misshapen as a gnome. Once a week, for years past, it had been Miss Penelope's custom to walk out to the Poplars, attended by Dennis, her man-servant, carrying a basket of home-made delicacies; oftentimes had Gay begged to be allowed to go with them, and to wait outside the door till her aunt's visit was at an end. Miss Penelope's foot alone was permitted to penetrate the dim hall with the stately fan-light over the front door, where she was received by her friend of childhood, Miss Selina Stith, the younger of the owners of the house. Dennis, relieved of his burden upon the steps, was glad to sneak away to the common opposite, where such cheerful every-day sights as geese stalking in a string, cows grazing, and boys wading in little pools, might restore his equanimity. Gay, less timorous, liked to stroll the round of the weedy carriageway with its iron posts and chains, shut off from the street by a high brick wall, and to gaze up at the rows of windows like dead eyes, at the chimneys whence arose so little smoke, at the dreary ivy that had overlapped and strangled every outlet of the melancholy house. When Aunt Penelope came out, it was always with reddened eyelids, and a cloud upon her usually smiling face.

"No better, Aunt Pen?" Gay would ask.

"No better, my dear child, and never will be this side the grave, poor thing," the good lady would reply.

It had been full twenty years since any one outside had seen the elder of the Misses Stith. More familiar to neighborhood eyes was Miss Selina, who sometimes, in the dusk of warm evenings, came out of the decaying mansion to wander wraith-like in the streets. The children of the mechanics who lived on the outskirts of the town were accustomed to the apparition, and, when she passed them at their play, gazed curiously after but did not follow the queer little figure in the garb of fifty years before—an "umbrella" frock with leg-o'-mutton sleeves, and a poke-bonnet draped with a veil of sprigged black lace.

Now and then she would pause beside some group at play, and two eyebeams of softest blue would penetrate the meshes of her veil and rest quietly on the little ones. Sometimes she produced from her reticule odd toys of an unfamiliar pattern, and silently laid them in the lap of some baby in a pet or neglected by its mates. But she never spoke, and as darkness closed would melt into the shadows of the night.

"I wish I could see Miss Selina face to face," sighed Gay, one morning, when returning with Aunt Penelope from the customary pilgrimage. "Major Garnett told me she was the prettiest girl that ever grew

up in Belhaven. He says when he was a lad, and
used to look up into the organ-loft of Christ Church
and see her singing, all in white, he called her St.
Cecilia."

"Yes, my dear; a beauty she was, and so gay and
merry—her paintings on rice-paper universally admired—and such a finger for the harp! It is one of
the mysteries of an inscrutable Providence why she
should have followed Celestia and become—ahem—
deranged."

"And, O Auntie, Peggy says the curse upon the
Stiths may one day be removed by a secret you know
of, but that I am not to be told. And I think, considering I 'm well past fifteen—do be a dear, and
tell me what it is."

"Peggy should certainly be checked," began Aunt
Pen, with a rather guilty blush, remembering a noc-
turnal gossip of her own with the old woman not
many days before.

"If I could only go inside the Poplars *once*," pursued Gay, plaintively. "Think of aching all one's
life to get behind a door!"

"Don't think of it, child. It is too sad for words.
There is nothing for you to see," replied Miss Pen,
with so woebegone a face that Gay dared not persist.

Everybody knew the old story of the Stiths. Just
before the American revolt against the crown, there
had arrived to settle in Belhaven the younger son of
an English family, a man handsome, winning, and
possessed of sufficient fortune to make people speculate as to why he came. Oxford-bred, and carrying
good credentials, he, however, speedily made for him-

self a place in the affections of the town, and married a beautiful heiress who was the toast of the countryside. Of the cause impelling Mr. Theophilus Stith's emigration to the New World, tradition said that it was a last effort to break the spell of a curse transmitted through several generations of his ancestors to the younger son of his family. Long ago, the English legend ran, there had been of this line a daring youngster, who in a fit of bravado pulled down a ruined chapel upon his estate and built with its stones a banquet-hall, in which, wine-cup in hand, he had been struck dead while reveling. Since then, no younger son born to the house of Stith had prospered. Belhaven doubters, and there were not a few to greet this myth with mocking, had in time to witness the dark close of a career begun among them under brightest auspices. Let Miss Penelope take up the tale as Gay heard it in her youth.

"Yes, my love; Mrs. Theophilus was the envy of the place. Her husband built and fitted up for her the Poplars, then well out of town; all the furniture came from England, together with a handsome new chariot to which she drove 'four' along the Rolling Road and elsewhere. For a while she was as happy as a queen. Children came very fast, and every corner of the house was full of young faces and voices — ten children had Mrs. Stith. Selina, my contemporary, was the youngest of the flock."

"Well, Auntie?"

"Oh, they had trouble; his habits were not good, I 've heard. One day his horse came home to the Poplars without its master; they picked up Mr. Stith stone-dead, and his wife's death followed shortly."

"And then, Auntie?"

"My dear Gay, you know it is one long tragedy. Every member but two of that gifted and promising household came to a sudden or tragic end."

"It is like one of the cycles of Greek plays, where whole families are swept away by death, that Dr. Falconer read me about in our lesson yesterday," said Gay.

"On poor Celestia, who with her sister alone survived, fell the burden; for she had been the little mother of the rest. She and Selina had their youngest brother Richard's only son to bring up, a handsome, wilful boy, called Llewellyn. Celestia was always a reserved, self-centered nature, but in her way she loved Llew dearly, while Selina lavished on him her full, warm heart. The lad had entered the university, and was doing well, when a dispute arose between him and his older aunt about some matter trifling enough, God knows, to have caused such dreadful results. Celestia was not happy in her way of dealing with the young. Llewellyn declared that he had rather go and dig in a ditch for his living than be dependent on her whims. I forgot to say, my dear, that by this time their fine fortune had melted like snow in the sun, and Celestia had much ado to make two ends meet. Well, Celestia bade him go, and, spite of Selina's tears and prayers, the boy left them one morning, and has never been heard of since — Gay, my dear, we are passing Slater's, and forgetting to match Sister Finetta's gray alpaca —"

"One minute, Auntie. Was it Llewellyn's loss that made Miss Celestia go insane?"

"Who can tell, child? From melancholy she passed

9

into utter aberration; and Selina, though, as you know, less grievously afflicted, has gone under the same cloud. Do you think it would answer to trim it with a piping of gray satin? Would sister think it too smart?"

"Let us pipe it 'unbeknownst,'" said Gay, smiling, "and she won't have the heart to rip it off. Auntie, I can't think Llewellyn Stith had really a good heart, or it would have softened in time to those poor women who loved him so."

"'He will come back,' Selina said, at first repeating it day after day. Then she ceased to speak of him, and, before her poor heart was broken quite, lapsed into merciful oblivion."

"Oh, it was wicked, cruel!" cried Gay. "How I should like to tell him so!"

"My dear," said Miss Penelope, mildly, "that was thirty years ago."


## II

In the autumn of 1859, to Gay, then a blooming lassie just beginning to find out her own good looks, occurred an event that in dull Belhaven had power to excite in her a temporary indifference to all human woe. Through an old friend of the family, a leader in the social world of Washington, she received an invitation to meet the party of the Prince of Wales on the occasion of his intended visit to Mount Vernon.

Although the visitor was only a lad, republican

maids and matrons along the line of his travels were palpitating to secure such an opportunity as came unsought to our little homespun Gay. To her, in truth, it was less prince, more outing. She had not learned the importance of a hand-shake from budding royalty under watch of a cordon of tutors and courtiers. Sufficient to fill her cup was the prospect of an entirely new frock made by Viney Piper, and a new ostrich-feather for her hat — one that might perchance — oh, thought of joy! — go entirely around the brim and rest upon the shoulder. Belhaven generally was content with simple tips.

"It is the Queen's eldest son, my dear, and we have always been fond of England," said Miss Penelope, fluttering. "I should n't wonder in the least if your Aunt Finetta should decide to unlock the wardrobe, and look up something of poor Lucilla's that you might wear."

Gay's eyes sparkled. She could never get over the thrill that ensued upon a hint of unlocking the wardrobe. But, in the mean time, there was the little sum set aside with careful consideration to purchase a new muslin, and new trimmings for her hat. And up King street, in Miss Pewee's window, she knew of a hat she meant to copy — the sweetest wide-brimmed Leghorn encircled with a plume of pale rose-color, and topped with a knot of rose velvet — a masterpiece of art. There could be no dawdling over the breakfast things that day.

As soon as Miss Penelope had "given out" supplies to Peggy and Susan, who with flour-measures and sugar-bowls and jugs attended her to the store-

room, Gay hurried the old lady into her bonnet and
shawl and away to the emporium of Miss Pewee, in-
tending afterward to repair to Slater's for the purchase of her gown.

"Let you look at that hat in the window? Why,
certainly, Miss Gay," exclaimed Eliza Pewee, cor-
dially. "You 'd best try it on, miss, for you can
never get an idea — I 'll vow, Miss Penelope, ma'am,
I 've yet to see anything set off Miss Gay like this."

Eliza, a member of Miss Penelope's Bible-class,
was well trained in fundamentals; she spoke honest truth. How could any one fail to perceive the
enchanting frame it made for Gay's waving locks
and dusky, long-lashed eyes, her rose-bloom and her
dimples? And, oddly enough, at that very moment,
a strange young man stepped into the shop inquiring
the way to the bookseller's, and, meeting Miss Gay's
brown orbs full on his, blushed, apologized, and retired in great embarrassment.

"Came down on the boat from Wash'n'ton early
this mornin'," explained Miss Pewee. "My sister noticed him when he got off. Seems foreign-like, don't
you think so, ma'am? Has been pokin' around town
all mornin'; quite the gentleman, I 'd say. Now,
Miss Gay, you really ought to let me send this home.
Day before yesterday, when I took it out o' the New
York packing-case, says I to Lizzie, it 's the very
thing for Miss Gay Berkeley — oh, no trouble in the
world, Miss Gay. I 've the same untrimmed, certainly; and feathers, too, only not half so long."

While Gay's reluctant fingers turned over the milliner's exhibit of raw material — while Gay, sorely

tempted, but aware that the price of the coveted hat would exhaust the money set aside for her complete outfit, tried to wonder how she could be satisfied with two tips and a ribbon bow instead of that lovely plume and the velvet sea-shell made by wonder-working fingers — Aunt Penelope was undergoing the same mental struggle. When Eliza Pewee, searching for the right shade, dived behind a curtain and disappeared back of the shop, Aunt Penelope cleared her throat, and spoke:

"Gay."

"Well, Aunt Pen?"

"My dear, I am not sure whether Sister Finetta would approve. I have always been partial to rose-color, and as this is the first time one of the royal family has visited Mount Vernon since the war, I think Virginians should make a little exertion. My love, *if* we buy this hat, what could be done about a frock for you?"

"O dearest Aunt Pen," cried the girl, radiantly, "let us have the old muslin washed."

As they were walking home — Gay in an *après-moi-le-deluge* state of mind — they ran again upon the strange young man coming out of the bookseller's with a parcel under his arm. They heard afterward (everything got about in Belhaven) that he had been trying to purchase any literature that might contain allusions to the early history of the town and its inhabitants.

"I suppose he is some young journalist from the North," said Miss Penelope. "Naturally enough, such people take interest in our town."

"His cheeks are as pink as my new ribbons," said Gay; "and he looks painfully shy and young. O Aunt Pen, you were a perfect darling to decide me about that hat."

And so the hat came home, was deposited in its bandbox on the Marseilles counterpane of the spare-room bed, was visited by Gay in her nightgown (to try it on again), by the Misses Bassett from next door, by Peggy and Susan and Cynthy from the kitchen, and in time became a proverb in the town.

On the day following, a family conclave gathered in the chill, speckless room wherein Great-Grand-papa Berkeley had given up the ghost, since in-habited in solitary state by his eldest daughter. It was a dusky chamber, with bed-curtains and win-dow-curtains of white dimity, the chief wall-space occupied by a massive wardrobe of lustrous mahog-any, before which, like a priestess at the shrine, stood the grim figure of Aunt Finetta, keys in hand. The wide doors of the sanctuary, yet obstinately shut, reflected Gay's rosy face, her dark brows puck-ered in a frown of intense expectancy, side by side with Aunt Pen's drab puffs of hair and scarcely less anxious visage. In the corridor outside, in an agony of curiosity, hovered a little black girl, who would have given a tooth or an eye to cross the threshold. With a rattle and a clank, Miss Berkeley unlocked the wardrobe doors and swung them back. Forth stole upon pleased olfactories a scent of attar of roses that changed, ere one fairly had sniffed it, into that of Tonquin bean; then a tang of camphor struck the air. They caught visions of squat band-

boxes covered with flowered wall-paper; of lac-
quered boxes, boxes of sandalwood, of Tunbridge
Wells mosaic, of Italian olive-wood, cabas and bags
of leather and satin, and of homelier green baize;
of parcels wrapped in rice-paper, in silver-paper, in
tissue-paper — all neatly ranged upon the shelves.

Gay's attention was fairly dazzled, roving between
Lucilla's Mechlin pinner and the waistcoat with silver sprigs worn by great-grandpapa to President
Washington's levee — between a pelisse of white
satin, painted with ragged-robins, and a "slip" of
pale blue trimmed with tarnished silver fringe, in
which Miss Finetta had danced a minuet with Colonel
Aaron Burr. She handled a necklace of turquoise
disks enframed in golden filigree, and let a long
chain of aquamarines glide rippling through her
hands, till recalled by an exclamation from Aunt
Penelope.

"Sister! While you have the writing-desk in hand,
suppose you let Gay see those miniatures of poor
Selina and Llewellyn she gave us on the boy's eigh-
teenth birthday. It is a long time since you had
them out."

"Is *that* Miss Selina?" cried Gay, eagerly. "How
perfectly lovely she was! O Auntie, there is no one
so pretty now. And this—why—how odd—Llewellyn is exactly like the young man we saw buying
books at Stringer's yesterday."

"My dear child," said Miss Penelope, catching
her breath, "you take me by surprise. It is hardly
a subject to jest upon. Put away the pictures, child,
and pray say nothing more about them. It is long

since I have cared to look at either. There, sister,
that is the organdie I spoke of—pink convolvulus on
a white ground—so beautifully sheer—if Viney can't
make it over for Gay, nobody can—pity it's a little
yellow. To be sure, the Prince is but a lad, and he
might not notice it is off the white."

But Miss Berkeley, standing erect and unsmiling,
the filmy fabric flowing from her arms, answered not
a word. She was thinking of the dead young sister
who in her brief season had been as full of the pride
of youth and the flush of hope as Gay. With a deep
sigh, she laid the dress in Miss Pen's lap, and when
she spoke again it was to utter some moral reflections
upon the duties and responsibilities of a prince, drawn
from the fount of her favorite classic, Dr. Johnson's
"Rasselas."

"Ting-a-ling-a-ling!" went the front-door bell. It
was before visiting-hours, and they knew that most
of the ladies of their acquaintance were making
pickles at the time.

The little black girl, fortified by a sense of duty,
knocked boldly at the chamber door. When bidden
to come in, her eyes wandered wildly on every side
at once, trying to take in all she could while delivering her message.

"It's ole Major Gyanett, miss; and he axes to see
de ladies mos' partic'lar."

"Penelope, you will go down at once," said Miss
Berkeley. "I shall follow when I have put away the
things."

Covertly adjusting her cap, Miss Pen obeyed. Gay
accompanied her to the blue parlor, where they found

the little gentleman walking up and down in great
excitement.

"God bless my soul! Miss Penelope, ma'am, here's
an extraordinary thing," said the old fellow. "News,
after all these years, of Llewellyn Stith, who is married and living in England, and has sent his only
surviving son to look us up. I'll declare to you
ma'am, that, in my hurry to let you know, I brought
my cane and forgot my hat!"

"One moment, David," said tremulous Miss Pen.
"You will kindly not tell me any more till my sister
comes down. My sister must be first to hear, of
course."

So Gay was the seeress, after all. She listened
with avidity to the Major's story when, Aunt Finetta
arriving, he was free to rid his burning tongue of the
strange tale. Llewellyn had gone to Australia in
his youth, and there fell in with a relative of the
elder branch of his father's family, whose daughter
he married, and who, called back to England to in-
herit a good property, was now succeeded by his son-
in-law. But although fortune had smiled on Llewellyn, he had known great sorrow. One member after
another of his family had died off, leaving only the
youngest son, Berkeley, named in memory of his
kind friends in Belhaven, whom he had never ceased
to love.

"Always the curse. I always said the curse would
not be lifted till the legend of the ring came true—
and oh! how can it come true?" interrupted Miss
Penelope, at this point, turning an eager glance first
at her sister and then at the Major.

Gay's ears and eyes opened. What, oh, what *was* the legend of the ring?

"Penelope, you will oblige me by not interrupting Major Garnett," said Miss Berkeley, frowning.

"Not knowing what members of our families still survive, Llewellyn, who is an invalid, directed his son to make inquiries through the British minister in Washington. Lord Lyons, who is my very good friend, referred him at once to me; and, after an effort to see me yesterday, when I was up the country, the boy returned to town to-day. It appears that poor Llewellyn feels that he cannot die without an effort to ask forgiveness of his aunts. Egad, ma'am, the trouble with me was how to tell the lad the condition of his afflicted relatives."

"Night and day since Llewellyn left her," said Miss Pen, tearfully, "Selina has worn around her neck a shirt-stud found on his dressing-table. Old Juno says she 'd as soon think of offering to take it off as of removing the ring from her Miss Celestia's finger."

Again the ring. Gay's mind was intolerably busy with speculation. Why had she never heard of it? In the midst of her wondering came the direful commonplace of a summons from Peggy, to know if Miss Gay was ready to begin on the pickled mangos. She waited to hear Major Garnett add that the lad, who was a pleasant fellow, but shy and awkward, had promised to return to Belhaven within a day or two, and to make him a visit until they could decide upon what to do in the matter of carrying out the injunction of his father.

"To look at young Mr. Stith, one would not have thought he came of such a cold-blooded, hard-hearted father," mused Gay, who felt that she had at last obtained her dues in the matter of a genuine romance.

### III

"It was a beautiful autumn day," said the newspapers of the time, "when nature put on her gayest livery to welcome to the burial-place of Washington the heir to the Georges' throne."

Gay and the Major, who was to be her escort on the drive, were in the hall of the house in Princess Royal street waiting for Timson's hack. The little Major, over his best auburn scratch, wore a well-brushed beaver hat, his blue body-coat was smartly buttoned, his standing collar was snow-white, his black silk stock was tied jauntily, and he carried his great-grandfather's gold-headed stick. Miss Pen, surveying him with lambent tenderness, felt that he was a credit to the day.

Gay, attired in Lucilla's organdie and Miss Pewee's champion hat, looked bewitching. Running out into the garden, she had picked for her belt a big bunch of "bleeding-hearts," and a smaller posy of the same for the Major's buttonhole. Now all was ready, and still the recreant Timson did not come.

"Tut, tut, tut!" said Miss Penelope. "I suppose he forgot to have the window mended that rattled so. Well, I always did say I could trust Viney Piper to cut anything; though she was unlucky with my

brown lustring a year ago last February, there 's
no denying it. How odd it seems for you to be going
to meet the Prince, child, when one remembers the
stand grandpapa took in the Revolution — though,
to be sure, grandpapa had fought *with* the English
in the French and Indian affairs. I must say it
shows a very proper feeling in the Queen to let her
son come. Dear, dear! if it should rain, if there 's
the least moisture in the air, I hope you will think
about your feather all the time, child! Mind you
take particular note of the color of his hair and eyes,
and remember all he says about the royal family.
Here 's good Miss Fanny Bassett, my dear, stepped
in to see you dressed. Yes, Miss Fanny; we think
our little girl looks very nice — Major, do you reckon
anything could have hap — there 's Timson at last,
and, I declare, if he has n't got the little white horses
with long tails that he drives to the baby hearse!"

Under the oak-trees on the Mount Vernon lawn
had gathered a pleasant company. The silver-haired
President with his fair, stately niece; Lord Lyons,
genial Sir Henry Holland, the imposing Duke of
Newcastle — these were most prominent in the *en-
tourage* of the blond boy with courtly manners, who
looked as if he would have liked to escape cere-
monial and enjoy Mount Vernon after some fashion
of his own devising. Elsewhere, everywhere, were
brilliant groups of fashionable folk, lighting up the
greensward to the semblance of a Petit Trianon. Gay
Berkeley, who had made her little reverence to the
Prince, had been rallied and flattered by some of the
oldsters of the suite, and was now followed by three

or four young fellows eager for her smiles, was enjoying herself with the true gusto of a Virginian belle.

When the little Major came up to her in the box-walled garden to present Mr. Berkeley Stith, Gay found it a decided interruption to her festivities to have to stop to "draw out" this reserved English boy, who colored to the eyebrows when she spoke to him. Romance incarnate though he was, Mr. Stith would have been more in place in Belhaven limits. Somehow he did not harmonize with her high-heeled Spanish *attaché*, or with the other glib and gilded youths who made up her train.

"Things are never quite what one expects them to be," mused the young lady, driving home, while the little long-tailed white horses, availing themselves of unprofessional opportunity, trotted briskly along. "It has been all delightful, but — but — I don't get on with Mr. Stith."

"He is very young," ventured the Major.

"That is n't it; I can always manage boys," said Gay, superbly. "If it were not absurd, I should say that he has some especial reason to be afraid of me."

"In that hat you are undoubtedly dangerous, my dear," responded the gallant old gentleman.

"No; but really, Major Daisy, I tried so hard. I told him everything I know about Mount Vernon — even the old story about the lady who wept over the ice-house, mistaking it for the tomb. But nothing would cheer him up."

"You will be better friends when he comes to stop with me," said Major Daisy, with confidence.

10

But Gay held to her opinion; and when, the next afternoon, she heard the door-bell ring, prepared herself for a dull quarter of an hour.

"I seen cote-tails on de fron' po'ch, miss. 'Spec' it 's students come to tea," said the little black girl, putting her head into Gay's room and irreverently alluding to the theological visitors most common in Belhaven streets.

"My dear, have you seen anything of my glasses?" said Miss Penelope, coming in with a card in hand. "O Cynthy, are you there? Run, look for my specs, child, and hurry if you can."

"Dey ain' no use hurryin' 'less Miss Pen hurry too," said the small dark person, pointing her forefinger at the old lady's puffs. "'Ca'se dar dey is, bof pa'rs, certain shua."

"It is Mr. Stith, Auntie," explained Gay, glancing at the card. "If you and Aunt Finetta are ready to go down, do you think I need come quite yet?"

"You will accompany us, my dear. I should like nothing to be lacking in our welcome of the child of an old friend who thought enough of my papa to name his son for him."

When the Misses Berkeley, all prunes and prisms and best silk gowns, entered the blue parlor, Gay in their wake, they found the stranger, holding his hat behind his back, inspecting the miniatures that hung in a row above the mantel-shelf. He turned, and, at the first look into his honest blue eyes, the two old women, seeing the unmistakable likeness to the long-absent Llewellyn, melted in kindness to the lad. Placing him between them on the haircloth sofa, they conducted the conversation in alternate rivulets of polite inquiry. Miss Pen, solicitous about his father's failing health, urged on him the propriety of sending at once to England a large supply of her Grandmama Berkeley's preparation of wild-cherry bark, tar and honey; Miss Berkeley, elaborately unbending, contented herself with propounding oracles concerning the British government, the aristocracy, the Church and customs of his native land. Gay, from her taboret in the window-seat, caught the humor of the scene. When, upon being pressed to say how the Queen was looking when he saw her last, Mr. Stith, turning his silk hat nervously, answered that "It was at a flower-show, you know, and her Majesty was rather hot, and uncommonly red in the face," Gay, observing the shocked expression of her aunts, burst outright into laughter that went trilling through the empty spaces of the house. At which Berkeley Stith's young spirit overleaped conventionalities, and he too laughed. Dennis, coming in with a salver containing cake and wine, relieved the situation for both the lawless ones.

From this date Berkeley was adopted as one of them. He lost his constraint in the presence of their simple cordiality. The pleasant house, with its bare, polished floors, wide halls, old-fashioned furniture and customs, the jolly negro faces in every background, the smell of dried rose-leaves everywhere, the soft voices, to say nothing of the rich Southern beauty of the little maiden who already had him in her chains, made life there seem an afternoon of holiday from school.

They had talked much of the ways and means of introducing Berkeley to his father's aunts. Miss Penelope, indeed, had urged upon the lad the hopelessness of attempting to rouse either of them to recognition; but when, with quiet determination, he assured her that it was impossible for him to return to England, having neglected the effort to do so, Aunt Pen agreed to second him.

Gay had never set foot in the garden of the Poplars. She had seen the horse-chestnuts flower and drop over the high brick walls, and the long arms of distorted fruit-trees let fall, outside, pears and plums too hard and warped for even the milk-teeth of eager children of the street; but all within was a mystery like the contents of the house. When Aunt Penelope, coming to meet them at a door set in the ivy of the wall, unlocked it to admit her with Berkeley Stith and Major Garnett, the girl looked about her, full of awe.

Nothing so dreary as this tangle of neglected vegetation had come within her ken. Elsewhere, at this season, in the gardens of the town, rioted a glorious second crop of blossoms, richer in tint and sweeter of smell than those of summer-time. Here, so long had nature unpruned laid one layer of growth upon another, the foliage underneath was skeletonized and gray. The few flowers that had struggled into bloom were touched with blight. The great old sycamores, mulberries and "paper-leafs" locked their boughs to make a twilight down below. Under the rotting arches of a grape-arcade there were two long tracks worn by footsteps, distinct as the "beat" of prisoners

in Old World dungeons, where, for half a century,
Miss Selina had taken her daily exercise.

"Now, my dear, keep your spirits up," said Aunt
Pen, in a cheerful whisper. "It will startle her
less, I think, if you and the Major come in with
Berkeley. Rain or shine, I've been visiting here this
many a year, and I've met with nothing more alarming than mice; so pray, all of you, put off those dole-
ful looks. I find from Juno that poor Celestia is
very weak, though she's up and in her chair, as
usual, in the room she's never left in twenty years.
My plan is to have you come into the upper hall,
where in old times the young people used to sit and
chat around the bay-window seat, and let Selina find
you there."

They mounted the stairs and sat, a silent trio, in
the half light that filtered through panes overgrown
outside with ivy. The paper of walls almost covered
with mezzotints and steel-engravings, now obscured
from sight by grime, hung in melancholy garlands;
the fiddle-backed chairs ranged in rows around them
were whole, but veiled in dust; across the open door
of a bedroom opposite a spider had spun its web in
full view. Another door was conspicuously closed.
Not a sound smote upon their ears in the great voids
of the silent house but their own quickened breathing and the buzzing of a bluebottle fly attempting
to escape to outer air.

"Oh, will Aunt Pen never come!" whispered Gay,
at last, and Berkeley, who was next to her, took her
hand in his, smiling at her wan looks.

The little Major, hat in hand, sat in a brown

study, his eyes fixed upon the ground. He was living over a lifetime of joy and sorrow, of which the young things near him had tasted only the first drop. Gay felt herself shivering closer to Berkeley, who kept her hand in his firm clasp, saying not a word.

And then, led by Miss Penelope, who, with her arm around her waist, spoke in a low gentle whisper in her ear, there came to them a small, slight creature clothed in white, her flaxen hair, streaked with gray, hanging upon her neck, her wide, sad eyes looking at vacancy.

"Here are friends who love you, Selina," said Miss Penelope. "Look, my dear, and see if you do not remember David. And this is my little Gay, of whom I've often talked to you; and this is —"

"Llewellyn!" cried the poor lady, a look coming into her eyes as if a lamp had been set into a dark casement. "Llewellyn, my own boy, you've come back to us at last!"

Berkeley Stith caught in his strong young arms the frail form that swayed toward him. At the same moment was heard from behind the door of the closed room a shrill scream, and old Juno, running out like a spider from its lair, appeared among them.

"O my poor mistis, she 's no mo'! My Miss Celestia 's gone!" she cried. "Bress Jesus, dere 's one on 'em he 's taken to hisself. She 's done passed away in sleep."

Miss Penelope looked in alarm at Selina's white face resting on Berkeley's shoulder, but it wore a smile of ineffable content. She had heard nothing, suffered nothing. The brief gleam of reason, giving her the desire of her heart for years, had faded, leaving her at peace.

Miss Selina made no resistance to the removal from her old home into a place where every care was lavished upon the remainder of her days. She was gentle, grateful, obedient; did not seem to realize her sister's death; and at a second meeting with her grandnephew showed no recognition of his presence. That she had, however, secretly visited the chamber of the dead, to remove from Celestia's finger a quaint ring of twisted gold, was proved by her last act before parting with Miss Penelope to go into her retreat.

"You will give this to Llewellyn, with our dear love," she said, laying the ring in her old friend's hand. "Celestia had been keeping it till he should come."

Berkeley could not trust himself to visit again the old house at the Poplars until the week after Miss Selina's departure. Already some people who had been put in charge had opened the deserted mansion to light and air; and with Gay the young man wandered through it, gazing curiously at the scene of the drama of death in life, so recently enacted.

"This will all be yours some day," said Gay. "I hope you will never let coarse, unfeeling people get possession of it, and tell its stories to gaping visitors."

"When this house goes from my hands, it shall go to destruction, if I have my way," he answered. "But I can fancy certain conditions under which I should even like to live in it."

What those conditions were Gay did not press him to explain; nor were they apparently realized, since to-day, running close to the site of the old dwelling, destroyed by fire during the war, a railroad intersects the garden, and rows of small frame-houses have taken the place of the tangled bowers where Selina was wont to walk.

But when, some years later, Mr. Berkeley Stith came back to America to claim a bride, the ring used for the ceremony was one of the odd "gimmals" of the seventeenth century, made of blended links held together by a pair of golden hands, which, when separated, allowed the circle to drop apart. Within were inscribed these lines:

"When — With — This — Round — Trew — Hartes — Doe — Wedde — Yᵉ — Curse — Shalle — Pass — From — Stith — Hysse — Hedde."

"So we are the legend of the ring?" said Gay, fingering it curiously, upon her bridal eve.

"Yes. At least my poor father, who in his last days took hold of the fancy with surprising persistence, made me promise to induce you to wear it at our marriage. I must own, however, that I believe in it just as much as I believe in our fabled curse, and as most people believe in their respectable old family ghosts."

"Take care! Peggy declared that it was this scoffing spirit on the part of the previous Stiths that brought about their woes."

"Our luck has turned since the day I saw the dearest little girl in the world admiring herself in a milliner's looking-glass. I'll own to you now, Gay, that

I fell so hopelessly in love with that hat that I was afraid to look you in the face next day, for fear of letting out my secret."

"Oh, I am so glad!" the girl cried gleefully. "To have been loved at first sight, and to be married with a legendary ring, realizes all my youthful dreams. I shall never be silly any more; but it is a final tribute to my foolish old romance."

If Gay had consulted Aunt Pen (then Mrs. David Garnett) and her husband, who gave the bride away, they might have told her that all of life's romance is not in the dreams of youth. But this, perhaps, in her happy married life, she has now found out for herself.

I

 FAIR May day in the spring of 1860 found two young men riding along a wood road of the border-land in Virginia, destined before long to echo with the ring of troopers' steel, with the tramp of hosts marching to war in mighty phalanx.

As yet, there was of the strife to come only a distant thunder growl in warning, and the ears that heard it were those of the watch-dogs of the nation! Hoyt and Newbold, formerly chums at college, had drifted hither in the course of a Southern journey undertaken after Newbold's serious illness at his home in New-York. Hoyt, wide-awake, blue-eyed, alert and unimaginative, the mercantile element in his blood kept in check by the veneer of gracious Fortune, wondered at Newbold's vagrant fancy for byways and odd corners during their agreeably aimless jaunt. He would chaff his friend without ceasing over his fondness for lingering in churchyards, or losing his eye-glasses in dusty parish registers, while taking hieroglyphic notes from some saffron page, dislodging for the purpose the filmy skeletons of veritable bookworms which had perished there, long since, of delightful satiety!

"And what if I love the seed-capsule and you the flower, Hoyt?" Newbold said, summing it all up. "You are a flower yourself, a splendid specimen, meant to bloom in the foremost *parterre* of our coming American Renaissance. Nature intended me for a nook or a niche somewhere, or else the bottom of a china jar set in a corner cupboard.

"I say!" Newbold continued, dreamily talking, "somehow or other, I feel at home down here on the threshold of a world that is neither New England, with her high-pressure life of invention, enterprise, smartness, and general good repair, nor yet old England, with her storied memories. I like to think. I'm not likely to encounter a rising capitalist south of the Potomac. I've a pet vision of these old grandees chipped out of colonial history, who will be found sitting beneath the umbrageous branches of their family trees, smoking good tobacco and sipping — what do they sip, Hoyt — Falernian?"

"For Falernian, read old rye," Hoyt answered. "Newbold, you are the most preposterous dreamer and dawdler. I don't see what you make it out of. Look at these mud-holes, look at those crazy fences! Houses tumbling to pieces, old hats stuffed into the cabin windows, the negroes along the road like scarecrows, their children little nudities. Not a decent farm-house have we passed in three miles back; nothing but woods, woods, woods, before and behind."

"One pardons any heresy in a hungry man," Newbold answered. "Cheer up, comrade! Think of what
that dear, delightful fellow, Conway, who took us to
his heart and club in Baltimore, promised us! A
typical old border mansion (which should be hereabouts), and, for host, a relic of the pig-tailed gentry of a century ago. Conway, who is an eleventh
cousin of these Hunters, felt himself quite free to
bestow on us a letter of introduction to them. My
knowledge of the topography of Fauquier County
is limited, but, from the directions given by the ho-
tel-keeper at Pohick, we must be somewhere near the
Aspen River, which bounds the Hunter property on
this side. What a bit of road for a canter, Hoyt,
this alley just ahead!"

They were off at a gallop through the long, green
tunnel, made by oak and maple, sassafras and hem-
lock, sweet-gum and tulip-tree, blending their boughs
in leafy communion. Vines of wild grape clambered
everywhere upon their stout-shouldered neighbors,
hanging out banners of close-woven greenery and
tassels of luscious bloom. Here the light of the
afternoon sun was filtered across the mossy ground,
and from the hidden bowers of undergrowth came
the song of many a sweet, unfrightened bird.

Beyond this dense tract of woodland, the road
came suddenly to a halt upon the steep bank of a
rushing yellow stream, churned to mad activity by a
recent freshet. In a thicket of pines, upon the opposite shore, stood a weather-beaten red cottage, apparently deserted, with door and windows shut. A
line stretched across the stream, and a rude attempt

at ferry-tackle directed attention to the flatboat secured at the farther landing.

The two travelers sat their steeds and exhausted every known species of war-cry, whoop and yodel, but in vain. No answer, no sign of life from the ferry-house. Only the mocking note of a crow, as he rose from a tree-top and sailed in tantalizing fashion across to the haven of their hopes.

"Confound the free-and-easy Virginian who undertakes this business!" Hoyt exclaimed, furiously flicking the mud from his trousers with his riding-whip. "It is all of a piece with the shiftless style of the neighborhood. Just let me get out of this box, and I'll expose him; I'll write to the papers about it; it's simply a disgrace to the State!"

Newbold had been sitting with slackened rein and dreamy eye, taking in all the candid beauty of an afternoon in spring in this remote and dewy spot. He started, looked at Hoyt, a quizzical gleam came into his eyes, and Hoyt laughed, albeit unwillingly.

Just then Hoyt, the more far-sighted of the two men, saw a slight figure detach itself from the black shadow of a belt of pines behind the ferry-house, and, followed by another, come running to the bank. These were a boy and a girl, it soon appeared, and a shrill halloo across the swelling flood gave comforting assurance of relief at hand. To the surprise of the spectators, the creaking hulk of the ferry-boat was at once boarded by the two children, and was swung out, not unskilfully, into the eddying stream.

"By Jove!" Hoyt commented, admiringly, "the girl is doing the chief part of the work. There's

11

pluck for you, and muscle too, Newbold!  Look at the heave of that current, will you!  Three cheers for the ferryman's daughter!"

Steadily the boat came on.  Three cheers were given with a will, and, for answer, they could see the girl nod her head in quiet recognition.

"This is no ferryman's daughter," Newbold whispered, as the boat touched shore.

She was about sixteen, slender and shapely.  Her hat, trimmed with an oak-leaf wreath, had fallen back from her flushed face, and now, her task done, she stood, her beautiful bare hands clasped lightly across her waist, her breath coming quickened by exertion. The boy, her comrade, was a handsome, spirited creature, a few years younger.  Both young people were of that luxurious type of beauty one sees on the mellow canvases of Lely and his fellows, having the rich coloring, the short upper lip that seems haughty when in repose, the cleft chin, the well-dilated nostrils ; and both were clad in clumsily made garments of striped blue-and-white domestic cotton.

"Now, mind, Pink, I 'm to ride your Bonnie Bess to-morrow, without the curb, for letting you have first turn," the lad exclaimed; and at once his fancy was taken by Hoyt's mare, who had begun to give every evidence in her power that she disliked boarding the ferry-boat.

"Let me get on her, *please*, while you lead her on, sir," he pleaded.  Hoyt laughed, and acquiesced.  Quick as thought, the boy was in the saddle and had gathered up the reins.  The mare entered a final protest by rearing violently, while her rider, deftly slipping from the saddle, stood, with one foot in the stirrup, neck to neck with the dancing beast. Before Hoyt could interpose, the mare had touched ground, and the boy was back again on his perch, a bright, wild gleam in his laughing eye. With some difficulty our travelers succeeded in obtaining permission to share the labor of ferrying the boat back.

"Well, if you want to," the girl said, with evident reluctance. "But Dolph and I so seldom get a chance. Old Stubblefield 's afraid papa will hear of it, I suppose; but we made him show us how. Stubblefield 's gone to mill, you know. Very few people come this way, and Dolph and I just happened to be in the woods over there when we heard you call. I suppose you came by way of Pohick ? "

Here the boy broke in eagerly, with a certain pride: "My sister has been to Pohick once, when she went to the springs with Aunt Betty Alexander. I 'm going some day."

Hoyt laughed his jolly laugh. Newbold smiled at the thought of the prim, sleepy little town upon the turnpike road, where the railway station and telegraph office seemed as much out of place as a staring new label on a worn leather trunk. "Each mortal has his Carcassonne," he murmured. And then came the bustle of getting ashore, of depositing the absent Stubblefield's fee in a long-necked yellow gourd hung behind a broken pane in the window of the red cottage.

"Now add one more to your acts of friendship," Newbold said; "put us in the road leading to Colonel Hunter's house — I believe they call it Crow's Nest."

Dolph's laugh made the echoes ring. " Why, that 's our house. You just keep along this wood road to the right for about three miles, and we 'll meet you at the red gate. Come along, Pink; it 's only a mile across the fields, our way. Let 's see who 'll be over that fence first."

They were off like a flash, and Newbold's eyes met Hoyt's.

"Original specimens of country gentry, are n't they?" Hoyt remarked. "I say, Newbold, it 's getting deucedly on into the afternoon for a man who 's had no lunch."

They plunged into the recesses of a cathedral-vaulted pine forest, and Newbold fell to musing and murmuring aloud.

" What did you say?" asked Hoyt.

"I was merely asking you a question."

"I did n't catch it."

"It is this," answered his companion:

> "Have you seen a bright lily grow,
>     Before rude hands have touched it?
> Have you marked but the fall of the snow,
>     Before the soil hath smutched it?
> Have you felt the wool of the beaver,
>     Or swan's-down ever?
> Or have smelt of the bud of the brier,
>     Or the nard in the fire?
> Or have tasted the bag of the bee?
>     O! so white, O! so soft, O! so sweet is she!"

" I call that a great many questions," Hoyt rejoined.

At the red gate Dolph was in waiting. His sister had gone on, he said, to announce their coming to his father. Both men breathed freer on emerging from the wide reach of dusky pine woods.

A low stone house, straggling along the summit of a bleak hill, was Crow's Nest. A square porch in front, built of heavy timbers; many small windows, set with greenish panes of glass; a stack of outside chimneys; and, on either side of the door, two grim cedars, whose long arms year by year grew more long and gaunt, until they tapped the garret window-panes. Such were the distinguishing features of this old Virginian house, around which hung an air of pensive melancholy, as if it had long since become resigned to settle down into the gray of declining years. The visitors looked in vain for signs of feminine occupancy, a muslin curtain or a flower-pot. All was chill, silent, and unsympathizing, quite out of keeping with rosy Dolph, who was then engaged in consigning their horses to a ragged negro groom.

"Pink scolded me," he said confidingly, as he ushered his guests within. "She said I never warned you about Black Jack."

"Black Jack! Is he a desperado who haunts your woods?" Newbold naturally asked.

"It 's our mud-hole," the boy answered innocently. "Just outside the red gate, don't you remember? You might have gone round, but it is right far to go round. I expect you 'd rather have come right on, had n't you? Black Jack 's mighty bad in the spring!" And he wistfully surveyed the nether garments of his guests.

The inner hall of Crow's Nest was long and narrow, the walls hung with fishing-rods, with guns,

with foxes' pads and brushes, with bows and arrows
rudely made. A few smoke-stained ancestors in red
coats, and their ladies in court-trains and toupets,
hung near the ceiling. Along the skirting-board was
ranged a row of men's boots, and a pair of antlers
held men's hats in every stage of disrepair. A half-
dozen smiling negroes jostled one another in the
background; and, starting from the wainscoting, it
would seem, appeared an odd, old-time figure, in
study-gown and cap, his hair worn in a queue, and
his wrinkled face lit with cordial welcome.

"Welcome to Crow's Nest, gentlemen," he said
heartily. "I am pleased to see that Black Jack has
let you off the worse for a little mud only. Black
Jack is apt to be formidable at this season of the
year. Come into the dining-room, pray, and take
something after your ride. You, Trip, go tell your
aunt Judy to hurry with her supper."

To present a letter of introduction seemed a mere
matter of moonshine in the face of such a greeting.
Our travelers were soon conducted to a chill dimity-
draped chamber, with a bed of state in either end of
it, where they found a small imp of darkness already
blowing up a shovelful of embers beneath some light-
wood knots upon the hearth. A couple of beaming
black boys were on hand to brush and polish, and
even Hoyt's reluctant spirit began to own the magic
of hearty welcome.

In a scanty room below, paneled with dark wood
and dotted with profile likenesses cut from sticking-
plaster and pasted on a ground of white, together
with faded Poonah paintings, pendent ostrich eggs,

"YOU WILL PLEASE HAND MISS HUNTER IN TO SUPPER."

and many a smiling miniature, they presently found
the daughter of the house. Pink had put on a muslin gown, and tied her truant locks beneath a scarlet
bow. She received the two men without affectation,
though a charming blush settled in each cheek. She
did the honors by showing relics of the days of
George and Anne that warmed the cockles of Newbold's antiquarian heart. In came the Colonel, in a
well-brushed suit of black small-clothes; and a clang-
ing bell announced the family meal.

"You will please hand Miss Hunter in to supper,
sir," the old gentleman said, with a quaint wave of
the hand. As Newbold obeyed, he fancied himself on
tip-toe leading out a partner to the minuet!

As in most Virginian houses, the dining-room at
Crow's Nest was the most habitable spot about the
house. The light came through a number of narrow windows draped in turkey-red. Doors opened
and shut continually to admit processions of small
darkies bearing offerings of smoking bread and
cakes. Over a porch-shed thus disclosed grew a lilac-
bush in full bloom. On the high mantel-shelf stood
home-made "dips," in massive silver candlesticks,
ready to be lighted when the late amber daylight
should fade. At one end of the long room stood a
sideboard covered with fine old silver plate. Cut-
glass decanters, containing certain mysterious golden
fluids, were open to every new-comer. Upon the
table was seen the inevitable ham, bronzed with baking, fragrant with cloves, drenched in a bath of old
Madeira. Grouped round it were broiled chickens,
corn-pone and sally-lunn, jams and jellies, and a

host of like dainties.  At the four corners stood silver jugs of cream ; and a brave array of blue Canton
china adorned the bare mahogany of the shining
board.  On guard behind his master's chair was an
old mulatto, Jupiter, who, having grown gray and
nearly blind in the service of Crow's Nest dining-
room, was still (after Aunt Judy, the housekeeper)
ruler of every festival, his children's children aiding
him in attendance at the table.  Behind the tea-board,
where reigned a large silver urn bedecked with the
drop-and-garland of Queen Anne's time, the young
hostess took her seat, having in waiting at her
elbow an old colored woman with a kindly wrinkled
face and clad in spotless homespun.  A spectacle
always amusing to Northern eyes was the hero of
the peacock's-feather fly-brush, a small, serious darky,
mounted on a three-legged stool, whose plaited twigs
of hair stood erect with awe at his own importance.

As the guests entered the room, a number of tall,
swarthy, black-bearded loungers rose up to give them
greeting.

"My sons, gentlemen," said Colonel Hunter, with a
wave of the hand, scattering the while a brace of
fawning hounds from about his knees.  Six of these
stalwart youths there were, ranging in age from eight-
een to twenty-eight.  Shy and slow of speech, awkward and low-voiced, these props of a decaying house
answered respectively to the names of Ludwell, Catlett, Peachy, Noblet, Bushrod, and Horatio.  Only
the family Bible knew how many additional high-
stepping titles were allotted to each.  The same chronicle bore witness to the fact that, at the outset of her

career, the sole daughter of Crow's Nest had been
made to stagger under the combination of Edmonia
Septimia Demoretta Fanshawe Crump! This burden,
thanks to her negro "mammy," had been speedily light-
ened to the infant sufferer.

"Come to its own mammy, den, my lamb! De Lawd
knows, she don't favor old miss, nor old marse nuther
—bress His name! My baby's dess as purty as a pink."

And the solitary Pink's petals had opened day by
day until her maiden fragrance filled the old gray
house.

Three years after Pink's arrival had appeared a
seventh boy. Despite his fair loveliness, rivaling that
of his sister, Mrs. Hunter seemed to take alarm at the
appearance of another recruit to her husband's line
of male successors. She had made jam and bound
up bruises and knit stockings for so many boys that
the vehement protest might have been forgiven her.
At any rate, she died at Dolph's birth, and was laid to
rest under a lean slab already gathering lichens in
the family burial-plot upon a neighboring hillside.

Dolph's name was a parental tribute to that ancient
fascinator, Mrs. Radcliffe — an abbreviation of Udol-
pho, of fame for mysteries. After bestowing upon
his last-born this mark of attention, the old gentleman went back to his books, finding metal far
more attractive in the rows of mildewed volumes —
yellow-skinned or black-jacketed duodecimos, six-vol-
umed editions of wearisome old fiction, dusty piles of
bygone magazines, all heaped on the shelves of a so-
called "office" in the yard,— a damp, low-studded
room, with a mossy roof garnished with stonecrop.

In this asylum, chiefly, what remained of old Octavius Hunter's days were gliding by. He was content to look at the theater of life through the large end of his glass. In his eyes, the world, outside of his inheritance of five thousand acres surrounding Crow's Nest, had subsided into vulgar commonplace when certain old-time luminaries in Virginian politics, most of them his blood-relations, had become extinct. To prattle about the past glories of his family, who were tide-water Virginians of the old, aristocratic, profuse class,— hand-in-glove with the noblemen sent over to govern the colony, and themselves descendants of a distinguished English line,— was the solace of his life. The fine old river-places, furnished and equipped with English luxuries at a time when Crow's Nest was part of a dense virgin forest, had passed out of the extravagant hands of Colonel Hunter's predecessors, and there remained to him only this remote lodge in the wilderness. Here he was content to dwell, reverting to the days of his gay bachelor life, when he was an ornament of the State militia, as also an active member of the Fraternity of Free and Accepted Masons in the neighboring town of Alexandria. Standing on the hearth-rug, his spindle legs in black tights a little separated, a silver snuff-box in his hand, his parchment face glowing with animation, the Colonel would discourse to you by the hour about how his grandfather rode to hounds with Washington, and how his aunt Betty had danced with the General at a birthnight ball. So in politics, the Colonel would have nothing modern. The consideration of party topics, just then agitating the broad extent of the United

States, was of far less moment than the action taken by Washington about the free navigation of the Mississippi River, or Jefferson's renunciation of his favorite Embargo Act. If, after repeated efforts, one succeeded in dislodging the Colonel from his archæological eminence and bringing him to the consideration of present events, "Egad, sir," he would say, "it's arrant nonsense. Talk about breaking up the Union that was founded by the General! It can't be done, sir. Of one thing you may be certain — Virginia, Mother of Presidents, will stand firm, sir. Did I tell you of that little anecdote my father had from Light Horse Harry Lee, about the General?" The Washington intimacy was a source of undying pride. The father of the present owner of Crow's Nest had been a pall-bearer of the great republican, and a brass-bound clock upon the landing of the stairs still kept record of the hour of Washington's death, the hands remaining as they had been set shortly after the occasion of that national calamity.

The Colonel had married late in life, and the claims of a numerous family had not greatly incommoded the quiet current of his thought. In those days children had a comfortable fashion of growing up for themselves, untroubled by the endless aids to progress requisite now. The boys hunted, trapped, and fished, took what learning they chose to receive from a threadbare tutor forming part of the establishment, declined the college course proffered them by their father, and developed — as we have seen! Dolph took to his book eagerly, and he and Pink and the tutor had long, delightful séances in the school-

room — a round-tower dependence of the house, with
stucco walls and a conical roof, dropped as if by
accident in the yard, near the dining-room door.

Pink's childhood was a happy one.  She lived
abroad outside her school-hours — the housekeeper's
scepter, dropped upon Mrs. Hunter's demise, having
been triumphantly snatched up by Aunt Judy, the
household autocrat.  Pink was put on a barebacked
horse to ride to water when she could hardly walk,
and soon after learned to climb trees like a squirrel.
The six big brothers were kind to both motherless
children, who formed the romance of their monoto-
nous lives.  They petted them, broke colts for them,
brought home trophies of the hunt for them, from
an owl's nest to a fox's brush, saved for them the
earliest nuts and persimmons, and, at Pink's bid-
ding, would smooth their ruffled manes and check
the rioting of their speech at times of family reunion.

Such was the circle at Crow's Nest, now recruited
by our two travelers.  Whatever curiosity they might
have experienced was soon merged into a solid enjoyment of Aunt Judy's good things.  A Virginian hot
supper, or "high tea," as it would now be called, was
a thing to be remembered !

"We missed the canvasbacks in Baltimore," Newbold said, with a sigh to their memory, even amid
such profusion.

"Very savory eating are canvasbacks," said his
host.  "But you must know the cook, sir.  'Let them
fly twice through the fire, and eat them when singed,'
was a saying of my maternal aunt, Mrs. Peggy Mar-

shall, of Bush Hill. No currant jelly or wine sauce,
either. Did you ever hear this little incident of General Washington's latter days, sir? He went once
with my grandfather into Gadsby's tavern in Alexandria. Gadsby met them, rubbing his hands, with
the announcement that he had just received a prime
lot of fat canvasbacks. 'Very good, Mr. Gadsby,'
rejoined his Excellency, 'Give us some canvasbacks,
a chafing-dish, some hominy and a bottle of your
best Madeira, and I 'll warrant you 'll hear no grumbling from us!' Ha, ha! Have a slice of this ham,
Mr. Newbold. Jupiter, hand Mr. Hoyt's plate. Come,
no refusal. Of course you must — a thin slice of
Crow's Nest ham never hurt anybody."

Jupiter handed the plate; and, in the act of carving, the Colonel held his knife in air, to explain how
to make a really good ham.

"Mo' waffles, sir," said a piping voice at the guest's
elbow. Newbold wanted to groan. The time for preserves and cream had not yet come, and already his
satiated spirit cried "Enough."

One who has encountered the pressure of Virginian hospitality knows that there is nothing for it but
to submit, body and baggage. Hoyt and Newbold
made a feeble stand against extending their stay at
Crow's Nest; but, betimes next morning, a cart
drawn by a large cream-colored mule and driven by
a negro lad (whose garments, made of guano-bags,
commended Smith's fertilizer to the public gaze), set
off in pursuit of their luggage at the tavern in Pohick. Thus beset, our travelers resigned themselves
to a fortnight's loitering. Hoyt, an enthusiastic

12

sportsman, found his chief amusement in the saddle, under convoy of the stalwart six, or in roaming the woods and fields. Newbold derived endless entertainment from the life, the place, the people. Dolph and Pink led him captive everywhere. Aunt Judy was proud to show her various departments of baking, brewing, poultry-raising, hog-fattening, spinning, and weaving. He had called upon the new calf of the red-and-white cow; he had seen Judy make her wonderful "beat" biscuit; he had rifled her quince preserves in company with his allies. He liked best of all, perhaps, to pass hours in the old "office." In this retreat, common to most Virginian houses, the uncertain light came through small panes of glass, shadowed without by a massive clump of box-bushes causing dusk to fall within at noonday, and affording sanctuary where Aunt Judy dared not pursue her fowls fleeing for their lives from block and hatchet. Above the door, where, entering, the visitor plunged headlong down an unsuspected step, grew syringas, gnarled and ancient, with hoary bark and sparse flowers. Sometimes a nest of young chimney-swallows, loosened by the rain, would fall upon the hearth, "piping" for human sympathy. Hounds wandered in and out the door; mice sported on the book-shelves; not infrequently a young heifer sauntered down the flagged walk to set her forefeet on the mossy step and fix her serious gaze upon the occupant. Here Newbold liked to sit, opening moldy envelopes, exploring mouse-eaten documents, some bearing proud armorial seals, and taking notes from a family correspondence extending back to the time

of England's merry monarch. The spring days glided
by, till, on the eve of their departure, Pink summoned
both her guests to a final round of "the quarter."
Here, a number of whitewashed cabins, each boasting
its separate patch of garden, growing corn, sweet po-
tatoes, tomatoes, onions, and cabbage, were embow-
ered in foliage and connected by a broad walk swept
as clean as the deck of a man-of-war. A pleasant
hum of business struck the ear. Through open doors
were seen wheels, looms, hat-plaiting, basket-making.
One or two negro patriarchs, with heads like ripe cot-
ton-bolls, sat blinking in the sun before their doors.
On the grass, on the walks, everywhere under foot,
were sportive pickaninnies clad in a single garment.
As the visitors passed down the line, smiles, bows,
curtseys, and cordial good-bys were showered upon
the young men, who had won a host of admirers in
"the quarter."

Newbold lingered behind the others, and looked
back. It was a fine elastic day, full of sweet, homely
smells from wood and meadow and fresh-turned fur-
rows of the earth,—a day when the air "nimbly and
sweetly recommends itself unto the gentle senses."
From the farm-hands, at work on the slopes bordered
by dark lines of pine forest, came cheerful sounds
mellowed by distance; in "the quarter" chattering
tongues were heard, with the crowing of cocks and
the clamorous joy of hens who had just acquitted
themselves of their diurnal duty to society. It was
all peaceful and pleasant enough. While Newbold
mused with regret over their approaching departure,
he heard a cry as if of pain from Pink, who, with her

two companions, Hoyt and Dolph, had disappeared
down a path leading to an isolated cottage. Newbold
quickly followed, to be met by all three of the missing young people, Dolph having his arm around Pink,
who looked pale and terrified.

"It is nothing," Hoyt explained. "We were idiotic
enough to go into that old witch's cabin yonder to
have our fortunes told; and the woman was either
drunk or crazy, I don't know which, and frightened
Miss Hunter with some of her nonsensical sayings—
that's all."

"Oh! no," cried Pink. "Aunt Sabra never was like
that before—never." And she shuddered involun-
tarily, clinging to her brother.

They had passed into the glen, a broad grassy valley, strewn with boulders of rock set in ferns, where
dogwood-trees in full blossom made a blaze of white
radiance in the shadow.

"Sit down upon one of these royal rocks," Newbold said to the young girl gently. "Tell me all
about your fortune-hunting, and we will laugh at it
together."

But Pink could not laugh. She looked from Hoyt
to her brother, but did not speak. Hoyt, strangely
enough for him, seemed to labor under a rare spell of
embarrassment. Only Dolph laughed, like the light-
hearted lad he was.

"All this because Aunt Sabra had what Mammy
Psyche calls the highstrikes, Pink. It is n't worth
worrying about. After all, I am the fellow to be wor-
ried, am I not, Mr. Hoyt?" and the lad looked up into
his friend's face with a trustful smile.

"Oh! but she said—she said," Pink found voice to whisper, "that Dolph was—walking—across—his grave!"

"And that *I*, since Miss Hunter is too polite to continue the prophecy," Hoyt added, "that I am to be the grave-digger, or words to that effect. Pray, Miss Hunter, don't let this stupid accident mar the pleasure of our last day at Crow's Nest. Dolph here has shown that he believes in me. Won't you, too, be my friend?"

To Newbold's surprise, the color in Pink's face, as she placed her hand in Hoyt's, deepened to burning crimson.

## II

THREE years later, in February of 1863, an officer of the Union army, representing a brigade recently stationed at Three Fork Mills, in the county of Fairfax, Virginia, accompanied by his orderly, rode into the half-deserted village of Pohick.

Railway communication with that enlightened center had long since been cut off. The inhabitants nowadays would have been as much startled by the sight of a locomotive as were the red men who first beheld one on the far Western plains. Many of the Pohick people had packed a few belongings and hastily gone over the border to share the weal or woe of the Confederacy. Those who remained would cower behind the closed green shutters of their frame-houses and listen to the clang of sabers in their one straggling street, not knowing whether this meant the advent of friend or foe — for the little town occupied debatable ground. Some days the people would wake up to see a splendid body of Union cavalry, all a-glitter with brave uniforms and polished steel, dash gallantly on and away into the dangerous region beyond; and again, be roused from their beds at night to give food and warmth to a weather-beaten band of ragged troopers in gray, who ate and drank like famished folk, who for nights past had slept by snatches when and where they could, wrapped in blankets on the snow, and for days had lived in the saddle, scouring their desolate outposts, with ears alert and hands on pistol-butt!

More than once had the main street of Pohick been startled by the flash of a sudden fusillade, prelude to a skirmish short and sharp. The good citizens watched with clasped hands and bated breath, and presently, when the tide of battle flowed back from before their portals, leaving stranded there its flotsam and jetsam of dead and wounded men, the sealed doors flew open, and friend and foe were borne within to be tended till reclaimed.

Newbold had been among the earliest volunteers for the Union, and his years of experience in the invading army, although spent elsewhere than in these well-remembered haunts, had pretty well prepared him for the reception his blue uniform might expect to encounter here. He had anxiously awaited an opportunity to ride over to Pohick and make inquiry concerning certain old friends; but the opportunity had been slow in coming. A lull in border hostilities enabled him to pursue his investigations with tolerable security, apart from the general possibility of a

stray Black Horseman's bullet. He had set out with
a strange excitement of spirit, amounting almost to
exhilaration; but the aspect of affairs throughout the
country where he passed saddened, then thoroughly
depressed him. There was hardly anything to recall
the ride of three years before. Nothing can so transform a landscape as the fall of timber; and here acres
upon acres of forest giants had been laid low under
the decree of war's necessity. For the most part the
ground was bare and desolate, but here and there
were thickets of noble trees degraded from their high
estate. Upon hillsides once crowned with handsome
homesteads or generous farm-houses were now mere
skeletons of framework, glaring with hollow eye-
sockets, and showing ghastly blackened fronts, round
which the bleak March wind swept drearily. Everywhere fences were gone, outbuildings had vanished,
fields and orchards were laid waste. The roads were
vast mud-holes, glazed with a thin crust of ice. Passing a forsaken camp-ground, he saw the earth in-
crusted with a curious mosaic a newly shod regiment
had made by casting away their ancient shoes on
breaking camp. For companions, during miles of
this melancholy expedition, besides his orderly, he had
only troops of crows, whose ominous note seemed a
warning of evil to come. Last of all in the list of
dispiriting influences were the unmarked graves,
seaming the hillsides, scattered in the valleys,— mute
records they, but oh! how eloquent of recent battle-
fields,—though, alas! only a handful beside the countless number of those that, from Shenandoah to the
sea, scar the green bosom of beautiful Virginia!

Newbold was not surprised at the scanty welcome
he received on drawing rein before the long piazza of
the tavern at Pohick. The hostler who appeared had
a gray look of chronic apprehension invading the
ebony of his once jolly countenance; and mine host,
who of old had swaggered out to meet and pledge
each new-comer, kept to himself behind the ill-sup-
plied bar counter, the tide of his courteous verbosity
curbed and leaking out only in necessary monosylla-
bles. The tavern folk, and those few who appeared
upon the thoroughfare, were all guarded, suspicious,
anxious, furtive. Newbold's hardly veiled eagerness
of inquiry for news of the family at Crow's Nest met
with evasive answers. They gave him such plain
food and drink as they could furnish, and left him to
himself in the long, chill dining-room, with its last
summer's decoration of fly-specked paper garlands
still pendent from the ceiling. Newbold's appetite
was not unduly tempted by the cold ham and scrambled eggs, the adulterated coffee and sharp green
pickles set before him. He rose up in a moment or
two and strolled out into the stable-yard to give an
order concerning his horse.

Here he was confronted by an odd object he
vaguely remembered to have seen before. It was a
crippled negro, old and bent, who, broom in hand,
was sweeping out the stalls. At Newbold's greeting, the old fellow looked at him, first curiously, then
with sudden intelligence in his eyes.

"I knows you, marse, shua 'nuff; but you 're
fleshier and more conformabler den you was. 'Spect
you disremembers Sam! You hain't forgot Crow's

Nes', has ye? I 'se Unk Pilate's brer, wha' ye gin a quarter to, de day ye sont me 'cross Black Jack to open de red gate."

Like a flash the time alluded to came back. Newbold recalled the race on horseback to which Pink had challenged him — the quaint old fellow gathering underbrush along the roadside. The warm balsamic air of the pine woods seemed to blow upon him. He saw again the perfect poise of her light figure in the saddle. Her ringing laugh echoed in his ear.

"Sam, you 're a trump," he said, with returning spirits. "Here 's a dollar to keep the quarter company. Now tell me all you know about the Crow's Nest family, and how you came to be wandering off here to foreign parts."

The old negro looked around him apprehensively, as his long claws closed upon the greenback, and, shuffling, he led the way into a disused stall.

"Mighty cur'us times dese, marse. Can't tell yer right hand w'at yer lef' han' 's scrabblin' arter, 'pears to me."

· Here he paused, coughed, looked wistfully into Newbold's face and, extending his lean forefinger, touched the young man's shoulder-strap.

"Ye would n' do no hurt, sir, to my ole marse, if ye does wear dis?"

"I would n't be fit to wear it if I did, Sam. I was a stranger and he took me in, remember," Newbold answered heartily. "Come, old man, out with your story. They are well, I hope. She — they have not been troubled in their home?"

"Dey 's only tol'able, Marse Newbole," Sam said,

scratching his head dejectedly. "When de wah fus' bruk out, 'pears like ole marse kinder disbelieved de news. He'd set dere in de office day in and day out, and w'en de papers cum twicet a week, he'd git kinder riled, and den 'pear like he forgit all 'bout it. De young masters dey kep' gittin' mo' an' mo' oneasy. Dey confabulated 'mongst deyselves — ole marse he kep' on disbelievin'— twel one mornin' de boys dess tuk an' lipt ober de fence, so to speak, an' jined de army ober yonder at Manassy Junction. Ole marse felt bad den, I recken, w'en he found dey wor n't nobody to fill de ole house 'cep' little mistis and Marse Dolph. He tuk to walkin' up an' down de flo', and dar''s whar he is now, I 'spec's. Little mistis, her eyes tuk to shinin' brighter 'n lightnin'-bugs, en she and Marse Dolph never rested widout dey knowed wot was goin' on in de camp. Dem two chillun 'u'd ride down to de Junction ebery chance dey got. Little mistis 'u'd keep all hands at wuk, sewin,' knittin' en cookin' for de soldiers. Dey wor n't nuthin' talked 'bout but marchin' and drillin' and paradin', en how General Beauregard was a-gwine to save de Souf. Bymeby cum a day wha nobody down our way ain't a-gwine ter forgit dis side de Judgmen'. 'T was hot summer wedder — de groun' a-bakin' wid de sun — and w'en we fust heerd dat rumblin' long de groun', bress your soul, sir, we tuk it fur de las' trump. Ef de fus' clap didn' bounce dat ole headen Si outen his cheer, en turn loose de wust skeertes' nigger on our plantashun!

"Den dey wuz mo' rumblin', en a lot of sharp cracklin' sounds way off to the norf of us. De fus' we know, dar was little mistis runnin' out in de sun widout no hat, en her cheeks as red as peonies. Marse Dolph followed arter her, and tuk her hand. Ole marse kem out en stood on the poach, lookin' like he walkin' in he sleep. De cracklin' set in louder den befo', en little mistis she screech right out to her par dat de battle was begun. She looked peart enough to 'a' fit herself, bress your soul; and de boy he stand dere wid his head up, en his ears cocked like a blood hoss w'en he hear a cone drop off de pine-trees. 'T was a mons'us hot day, Marse Newbole; en w'en night kem nobody on dat plantashun dars n't go to bed a-waitin' fur de news. Bymeby a sojer rode up de wood road. He sot his hoss sorter droopy, en w'en one o' de boys run down to de hoss-block, dar it wuz Marse Noblet's own sorrel, and dat wuz Marse Noblet ridin' him. He med out so ez to walk to de poach, wha old marse kem out to meet him. Den Marse Noblet bruk down like a baby, en if Unk Jupe had n't bin dar to ketch him, he 'd 'a' tumbled flat. 'De res' ob 'em is safe, father,' wuz what he med out fur to say, sir, ' but I 'se hit in de side,' en den he fainted, en we kerried him into de charmber wha ole miss useter sleep, en dere he died fo' mornin'. 'T was de blood-flow det finished him, de doctah 'lowed. Dat wuz only de beginnin', sir. Marse Noblet died o' Saturday, en o' Sunday de noise o' de guns begun ag'in bright en arly; en all day it kept rippin' en tearin' like mad. Ole marse set wid his head on his bre's' by Marse Noblet's body, en dem chilluns did all de orderin' dey wuz to be did. Sun up, nex' mornin', shua ez you baun, sir, ef dar wor n't one o' dem sort o' sick hearses a-turnin' in de red gate;

en w'at you s'pose in it? Marse Bushrod en Marse
Catlett *bofe,* sir. Dey wuz shot dead a-fightin' side
by side."

Sam paused, gave a gulp, of which he tried to seem
ashamed, while in spite of him two large tears ran
down his cheeks. These he quickly brushed away,
using a wisp of hay for the purpose, and resumed his
story.

"Well, sir, Mammy Lucy she laid 'em out, en we
buried dem free alongside dere ma in de cedar patch;
en little mistis she sont into Pohick en bought some
black stuff en had Mammy Psyche make a frock fur
her. Ole marse quit readin' den, en tuk to walkin'
up en down de flo'. Marse Dolph he seemed fit to
bu'st, kase ther' wor n't no chance fur him to git inter
de scrimmage on his own account. He en little miss
could n' ride about like dey useter, w'en de Yankees
begun to scout aroun' permiscus; en dey was fearful
restless en oneasy. Dar ent no use in me tekkin' up
your time, Marse Newbole, wid tellin' you all 'bout de
way things got a-runnin' down on de old plantashun
de secun year o' de wah. Arter de young marsters
quit, dere wor n't nobody to run de machine. Ole
marse got one oberseer, a po' white from de Cote-
House, en he stole en cheated; den anudder feller, he
cheated en stole. Bymeby, hog-meat gittin' skerser,
craps failin', ole marse sent fur all han's to 'semble in
de yard. Dar wuz we, in our Sunday bes'; dar wuz
he in dat ole study-gound en his little cap; little mistis behine him, all pale en showed she 'd bin a-cryin';
Marse Dolph holdin' on to her, en whisperin' now en
den. 'Boys,' ole marse sez, speakin' particular to

Pilate, Jupe, en me, cos we wuz de oldest, 'you all see how 't is wid me. Ye 's sarved me true en faithful, en it 's powerful hard to say it, but I hain't no call fur to starve my father's people, en so I 'll give ye leave to go. We 're dat near to Wash'n't'n it 'll be easy fur dem as wauts ter to git through de lines. Dem as has families to take wid 'em I 'll give a little money to start 'em on de way, en what I can I 'll do fur all on ye.'

"Dem niggers acted mighty queer, Marse Newbole. It cum as nateral as breathin' to want to holler out at dat. Dat wuz *freedom*, sir, dat wuz! But de sight uv our ole marse standin' up in de ole poach so feeble like, en dem po' young things behine him, wuz mo' stronger; en we jist kep' still as if it wuz in preachin'! Den Mammy Psyche gin de fust wud by squealin' out en throwin' her arms aroun' dem two, Miss Pink en Marse Dolph, en prayin' ole marse, for God's sake, not to send her off from her lambs, her precious babies. Ole Unk Jupe put his hand on one o' de do' poses, en he sez: 'Tek dis 'ere away, marse, but leave ole Jupiter.' En dat sorter bruk down de cer'mony ob de 'cashun. De wimmen folks en de chillun cried en hollered, en de men stood on de groun' ez if dey wuz bin havin' der dogger-types tuk."

Again Sam had recourse to the wisp of hay. Newbold stood in silence beside him, his eyes fixed upon the ground.

"I 'd like to tell you 'bout little mistis, sir," the old negro said, confidingly, after a time. "She waited a minnit to see cf her pa wuz gwine to say enny mo', en, seein' him settle down like he wuz dreamin', she

13

dess run out ou de grass amongs' us, sir, wid dat
same face she had w'en she wuz a-listenin' to de guns
at Manassy; it wuz proud, and den ag'in it wuz n't.

" 'I wornts you all to know dat my father en my
brother en I loves you jes' ez well en trusses you jes'
de same ez ever,' war what she say; 'en ef any one
'mongs' ye wornts to stay en share our poverty, he 's
welcome; en ef any one of ye wornts to come back to
Crow's Nes', he 's welcome. I 've growed up here
'mongs' ye, en I knows ye, big en little, ole en young.
It 's like pullin' my heart-strings out to see ye go
away, en de ole place go to ruin. But ef it 's got to
be, my dear, dear frien's, I know you 'll help — '"

At this point of his narrative, Sam made no further
attempt to stem the current of fast-welling tears that
streamed down the channels of his withered face.
Presently he abandoned the wisp of hay as inadequate
to the occasion, and took from his pocket a handkerchief emblazoned with the United States flag in all
its bravery of colors.

"Dat was de beginnin' uv de end, Marse Newbole,"
he said. "De Crow's Nes' niggers cl'ared out arter
dat, do de mos' ob 'em was mighty hard to stir. Unk
Jupe and Mammy Psyche dey staid, uv co'rse, en
dey kep' a couple o' boys to hope in de gyarden.
Aunt Lucy she went off to nuss in de hosspittle at
Culpepper. Aunt Judy, — she dat wuz housekeeper,
sir, — why she 's cook at Marse Secertary Chase's, dis
minnit, in Wash'n't'n, en Unk Pilate, her husban',
he drives de kerridge. Ole Unk Si he tuk his savin's
en made tracks, fust off. Hain't nebber heerd o' enny
cullud gentleman wha 's runnin' fur Presiden', down

dar, has ye, sir? De way dat nigger baambilated off,
ye 'd 'a' thought he wor n't gwine ter 'low Marse Lin-
kum no chance, nohow. Sum' on 'em has writ letters
beggin' marse to take 'em home ag'in; some on 'em
we ain't never heerd on. I 'm a kyinder old tarrypin
myself; en w'en little mistis 'vised me to be a-movin',
I dess crawled dis fur, en 'ere I stopped. I gets my
cawn-bread en my bacon en a bed to sleep on by de
wuk I does fur Marse Jim Peters, wha' keeps dis 'ere
hotel; but dey 's a mons'us differ'nce. 'Pears like I ent
got no self-respec', to be waitin' on po' whites, nohow;
en de longes' I live, sir, I ent nebber seen money tuk
befo' fur a stranger's bode en lodgin'."

Thus far Newbold had heard without wishing to
interrupt the simple old narrator, but a great longing
to know more of her toward whom his heart had been
drawn during years of separation overmastered him.
He wrung Sam's hand, greatly to that worthy's astonishment, leaving in the horny palm another greenback — an act of beneficence that almost defeated his
object by depriving the now smiling negro of his
powers of speech.

"Your young mistress, Sam, how does she look?
how does she bear her changed fortunes?"

"She 's grow'd like a hickory saplin', Marse Newbole, en it 's dess a wonder her sperret ent bruk, wid
de pore eatin', en de worriment, en de hard work. I
ent tole you, sir, dat Marse Peachy got killed at Mal-
vern Hill, en Marse Ludwell lay down dere in the hosspittle at Richmon' all las' summer, 'fo' he died o' de
wounds he got at Seven Pines. W'en Marse Raish
kem a-limpin' home on crutches wid one laig gone, en

took to settin' on de back poach all de day (underneath
de water-bucket wha de gourd hangs, sir, you 'members it?) en giv hisself up to bein' drefful onsperreted,
seems like dat wuz de las' straw! Ole marse looked at
him kinder fur off, en he sez, sez he, 'I 'm a' old tree,
en dey 've lopt off all o' my branches; purty soon de
trunk 'll fall, please God.' Den Marse Dolph en Miss
Pink dey tuk de whole fambly in charge. Marse Raish
allus was de perjinketes' ob all de boys, en he 's give
'em lots o' trouble sence, en old marse 'pears to git
childish like. Dat boy Dolph ez only fifteen, sir; but
ef you 'll b'leeve me, he 's breakin' his heart to go
enter de wah; en Miss Pink she wornts de wust way
ter please him, en but fer his pa I b'leeve he 'd be off
like a shot. . . . Dey 's powerful po', sir," he added, with reluctant admission. "All dat lan' 's no
good to marse; en de Yankees hez cut down acres uv
his timber. But dey 's great folks still, sir. Dey 's
Hunters, ebbery inch; en dey don't gib up."

NEWBOLD rode back to headquarters, turning over
in his mind a variety of projects by which he could
bring himself into communication with, and if possible aid, the family at Crow's Nest. A day or two
afterward, he met his old friend Hoyt, now captain
of New York volunteers, and, like himself, recently
stationed in the Three Forks neighborhood. They
dined together at Newbold's mess, and after dinner
Newbold resolved to make an effort to break an awkward kind of reserve that his own feeling had established between them in regard to the visit at Crow's
Nest. He gave Hoyt an outline of Sam's story.

"By Jove, it's too bad," Hoyt responded heartily. "Of course we should do something; but what? Our hands are tied. Very likely they'd bar the door against us, and the girl would hurl secession eloquence at our heads from the upper windows. What a pretty creature she was, Newbold! Do you know, I believe my wife is to this day a trifle jealous of the spooney way I used to go on about old Virginia after our visit there. I sent Miss Hunter a lot of books and engravings, and wrote her a half-dozen rather sentimental letters from Europe that summer — and there the thing cooled off. You remember, it was just before I became engaged to Lilian —"

"I have n't forgotten anything about that time," Newbold said, with a sort of effort. "Perhaps I never told you, Hoyt, that I myself fell as irretrievably in love with Miss Hunter as an idiot could. I wrote and told her so, and asked her leave to revisit Crow's Nest in a different capacity. But —"

"She did n't agree with you, old fellow?" Hoyt said serenely. "Well, that's a chapter that comes in most of our lives, is n't it? I am so well set up in that matter that I can afford to sympathize with you old bachelors."

"Unfortunately, as you will agree," Newbold added, after a moment's deliberation, "I have a provoking way of not changing when I once make up my mind. I find myself to-day more than ever fixed in my regard for her. The story that old darky tells of her pluck and her endurance has filled me with a rash and unmanageable desire to go to her rescue."

Hoyt whistled.

"Excuse me, old fellow, but really — I — It's such an immense joke, don't you see? Why can't you have the common sense to know that now she would never look at you? These Southern girls are the very devil! Perhaps you 'd better try it, though, if you are going in for a cure; or else wait awhile till we have settled this rebellion business, and affairs assume a different complexion. For my part I stand ready to do the Hunters any kindness or any courtesy that may be possible, if a chance presents. How Lilian will laugh when she hears I 've run upon the Virginian flame again!"

Once again upon the banks of the Aspen River our two friends came to a halt. This time it was no May-day pleasuring beneath the flowery arches of the wood. Hoyt was in command of a scouting expedition, which Newbold, out of the very restlessness of his spirit, had volunteered to accompany. The long winter of inactivity made an opportunity like this a godsend to both men and officers. It was now toward the end of March, and, by one of the coquetries of Virginia's climate at that season, a brisk snow-storm had set in, driving Hoyt's party into the shelter of a close growth of pine-trees for their noonday bivouac. Gathered round a tiny fire, whose thin blue curl of smoke they would have hidden from outside observation, they sat eating and chatting merrily—their horses, tethered close at hand, comfortably munching provender beneath a thatch of snow.

Suddenly the soldier on guard without gave a note of warning to his comrades. In an instant every man's hand was on his rifle. In the dead silence that ensued, they could hear the long, even stride of horses galloping on the far side of the river-bank. From their ambush they saw a party of Confederates emerge from the undergrowth opposite and sweep down the steep descent to the ford. Their steeds plunged into the stream and rioted with the swift yellow current, wading breast-high, now swimming, again striking bottom, and so until the hoofs of their leader struck the shore immediately beneath the wooded height where lurked their foe.

What followed was the work of a moment. Newbold, looking out with a thrill of eager anticipation, saw the graycoats fare gaily forward to their certain doom — saw in the midst of them, first to breast the current, waving his arm aloft in boyish pride — joyous, gallant, and alert — good God! could this be little Dolph?

"Fire!" came the ring of Hoyt's clear voice; and the order was instantly obeyed.

Newbold was conscious of a mad movement of protest. Before the smoke attending the deadly volley had scattered, the ranks of the rebel cavalry were seen to split asunder. Two or three bodies plunged heavily from their saddles to the ground. In the skirmish that ensued the rest of them, surprised and outnumbered, made desperate fight in vain. Those not slain or captured on the spot turned back to cross the ford, a rain of bullets following. More than one succeeded in crossing unhurt; some sank wounded on the far bank; and one poor fellow, struck in midstream, sat his horse gallantly until he had well nigh mastered the buffeting of the flood, then, falling like a column, was lost to sight beneath the angry tide.

It was short work to look for Dolph. The boy lay by the roadside, his fair face looking heavenward, a bullet through his heart.

Hoyt, having a severe thigh-wound for his own share of the encounter, was carried by his men into the shelter they had recently quitted and laid on a bed made of leaves and blankets, while a messenger, accompanying the prisoners sent back under guard, was despatched to headquarters in search of a surgeon. Into this retreat, where the wounded of both sides were lying, Newbold had caused Dolph's body to be borne. A faint hope, too soon extinguished, nerved him to continued efforts at resuscitation. Hoyt, on discovering the object of his friend's solicitude, was beyond measure shocked and grieved. In the intervals of his acute attacks of suffering, he would ask impatiently if nothing could be done to save the boy. From one of the wounded Confederates Newbold ascertained that this was young Hunter's first military service since his recent enlistment; and that the party, at his request, had stopped overnight at Colonel Hunter's house, whither it was more than probable some one of the retreating men had even now borne the news of the lad's fate.

"But I reckon I'd rather be here as I am, than in his boots that tells the news," the soldier added, between gasps of pain.

Newbold, having done what he could for the sufferers, paced up and down the road in front of his improvised hospital, a prey, for once in his life, to

blank uncertainty. As he strode back and forth, a
soldier on the outpost signaled him, pointing in the
direction of the far bank of the river. Going down
the steep path, Newbold saw through the mist of
swiftly falling snow the black hulk of the old ferry-
boat push out from the opposite shore.

"There are only two people aboard, sir," the sentry
said. "They've a white flag up. It's a woman and
a nigger man, I guess."

Newbold's heart was filled with foreboding. He
could make no answer; he could only watch and
wait. The boat drew nearer. What he feared was
realized. A gaunt old negro handled the ropes of the
ferry-boat, and at his side a young girl stood direct-
ing him. A moment more, and Pink, her large eyes
fixed and staring, no tear upon the whiteness of her
cheek, sprang to the shore and came swiftly up the
bank.

"I have come to claim my dead," she said, in tones
so strange and sad that, instinctively, every man who
heard her doffed his cap and stood bareheaded in the
snowflakes. Newbold dared not answer; he could not
tell whether she recognized him or not. In silence he
led her, followed by old Jupiter, whose shambling
steps found it difficult to make a footing, along the
slippery path. Dolph's body had been removed a
little apart from the others and laid on the moss at
the foot of a tree. Newbold hesitated for a moment;
then, drawing aside the sweeping bough that veiled it
from their sight, he motioned the young girl to pass
before him. He saw her swoop downward, like a
mother-bird to its young, and then could look no

more. She came out presently, the same marble creature who had entered there. Hoyt had aroused from
his benumbed condition, and, dimly comprehending
what had come to pass, begged Newbold to call her to
his side.

"I must say—a word—you know. She may feel
more kindly to see me—in this state."

He had raised himself upon his elbow and looked
appealingly toward her. Pink's eyes met his. To
Newbold's utter surprise, the young girl's face kindled with a momentary glow that was astonishment
and joy and tenderness combined. She made a quick
motion in Hoyt's direction, then as suddenly put both
hands before her eyes and drew back.

"Pray speak to him, Miss Hunter," Newbold urged,
in a voice that did not seem his own. "He is badly
wounded, as you see, and your—sorrow—is the one
disturbing thought he can't dismiss from his wandering brain. Surely, you will be merciful; surely, you
will believe that this terrible day's work was one
neither he nor I would have intentionally wrought."

As he spoke, the girl trembled pitiably; through
her clasped hands he could see a stain of vivid car-
mine dye her cheek, then vanish, leaving it pale as
before. With sudden impulse, she crossed to Hoyt's
side and bent down to him; but the wounded man,
exhausted by his effort, had already fallen back in a
stupor that might mean death.

Pink knelt for a moment gazing at him; then, rising,
turned away. Newbold caught the murmur that escaped her lips.

"Better so," she whispered drearily.

"Better so," he echoed in his heart. "She will perhaps be spared a deeper pang."

Dolph's body was wrapped in his soldier's blanket; but, when the moment came to bear him forth, Newbold and the men who offered to assist were motioned back by the lean arm of Jupiter, who, mute and solemn, had kept watch beside the dead.

"I ax yer pardon, sir, but dis is *my* place, and I has my mistis' orders," the old man said; and, lifting the body tenderly to his breast, he walked with majestic tread along the path—the girl, erect and tearless, following.

A cloth laid over the boy's face fluttered back. Those who in silent awe looked after the sad procession till it passed from view saw the gleam of his golden curls nestling in the protecting arms of Jupiter, even as the ferry-boat pushed out from shore. Midway in the stream Newbold caught his last glimpse of them: the girl at her old place by the ropes, battling with wind and current; the negro, on his knees beside her, striving to shield his burden from the storm. Then a mist came over the watcher's eyes; that and the falling snow blotted her forever from his sight.

.     .     .     .     .     .     .

A LITTLE while ago, Hoyt's young daughter, an airy fairy Lilian of seventeen, asked her father why their friend Mr. Newbold had never chanced to marry.

"He seems so solitary, papa," she said, from her favorite perch on the arm of Hoyt's library chair; "and sometimes, when he is here and we are all so happy, I can't help fancying it makes him sad to see us. I should like him to be happy too, papa; for he is the kindest, truest —"

"Yes, that is it, Lilian. If such a thing can be, he is too true."

And there, in the twilight, Hoyt told to his darling the story I have told to you.

# UNA AND KING DAVID

## I

T the close of a warm day of Southern spring, a little girl, most fair and delicately made, knelt at a window looking to the west, resting, in cherubic fashion, her pretty chin between two snowflake hands. A soldier on guard over a headquarters tent in the sun-baked space below looked up at her, and saluted gallantly; at which act of homage a smile broke over her face that was both tender and triumphant. Una was accustomed to such recognition from the men to whom her casement, with the flower-box nailed below it overflowing with geraniums and featherfew and mignonette in bloom, was the one bit of esthetic beauty in an arid spot. King David, an ingenious old artificer, had constructed for her this hanging garden from a box in which cork legs had been sent to the hospital camp; and, covered with bark from the neighboring woods, its appearance in public was now all that could have been desired. Through the monotony of hospital life, she ran like a thread of gold. When the little white-frocked maiden appeared in

**14**     157

the wards beside the tall and somber form of her
mother, who was a matron in charge of a division of
the camp, smiles formed upon wan lips, dull eyes
kindled, fretful voices were toned to courteous speech.
And, in return, she loved the patients as she loved the
cause for which they had been stricken down; fervently, unquestioning, as good Catholics treasure the
contents of their reliquaries. It was one of the pathetic things of that war between North and South
to see young spirits charged with such a burden of
fierce antagonism — young veins thrilling with a
fever of strife they could not understand and sought
not to remedy. And this our little Una, like all the
rest of them, was so terribly in earnest in calling herself a Confederate.

The place known as Camp Winder was situated
beyond the town limits of Richmond in 1864. Encircled by a trench yielding too often noxious odors,
the rough wards and tents were assembled in dreary
rows around a barrack of new pine boards, built after
the unostentatious model of a toy-shop Noah's Ark.
One expected to see the roof tilt back upon insufficient hinges, and the surgeons, matrons and nurses
for whose use it was constructed come tumbling out
like so many button-headed Shems and Hams and
Japhets. This drear abode, a honeycomb of hospital
industries, served as shelter not only for Una Eustis and her mother, but for many another of their
class born and bred in the lap of abundant comfort.
The unplastered room allotted to the division-matron
had contained until recently, for all furnishing but a
couple of army-cots, a table with washing apparatus,

and a few nails in the wall. Then, Fortune, in the shape of old Miss Jessie Sprigg, a spinster friend, who going to board in the country had nowhere to store her belongings, smiled upon them broadly. Claw-footed tables and chairs, a glazed bookcase and desk combined, a Chinese screen, and above all a comfortable lounge, arrived to transform the bare chamber into the semblance of a home. Una, with fairy fingers, had only to-day put to it her finishing-touches in the shape of a curtain and table-cover, and now waited, watching the red ball of the sun sink behind the pine grove westward of the camp — for at sunset King David would be free to come and take his sovereign lady for a walk. Her mother she might not expect to see till after supper was distributed to the sufferers, and the matrons and helpers were ready to sit down to their own meager meal in the refectory below.

Spite of the long, hot lonely day whose pink stillness of dawn had been rudely broken by guns at a distance, Una had, in her congenial toil, almost forgotten to be sad. Hour by hour since the morning round with her mother in the wards had her busy fingers sped. She could hardly be patient now that all was done. King David would never see how she had looped her curtains with her old blue sash. She longed to bring that faint gleam of a smile — so rarely seen now — into her mother's beautiful brown eyes.

The sun sank behind a blot of inky pines, casting up a fountain of radiance to the sky. A sudden pang of remembrance shot into Una's heart. The scene

recalled to her a vista in the forest surrounding her
old home — a spot where she, with papa and Hal, on
horseback, had once stopped to watch a similar effect.
She could almost smell the fragrance of dead leaves
and living mosses always arising from the deep Mount
Airy woods. She saw again a cheerful picture of
plantation life when the day draws near its close;
cows marching to the milking-place; chickens and
turkeys fluttering to their roosts; the black people
slouching home to the quarter, always ready to stop
for a pleasant-spoken "Howdy'e, Marse," "Howdy'e,
little Miss." Soon lamps would send forth their gleam
from the Great House windows, and the wide front
would be traced in light. What joy to spring from
the saddle by aid of Hal's young arm, and to go in
chattering and laughing with him to the tea-table
where the mother sat, and where the father would
come in to lend his buoyant presence!

So many people had their troubles in those days,
that Mrs. Eustis's recent share in the tragedy of war
had already passed into Confederate tradition. It was
hard for the poor lady, looking down at her frock of
coarse black stuff, and about her at the sordid belongings of her present life, to realize that she had been
the petted mistress of a fine old colonial homestead
on the Virginian border, forsaken at the outbreak of
the war to follow her husband's fortunes in the field.
The one visible link — after Una — to connect her
with that time was the diamond glittering upon her
finger above the wedding-ring, worn now, alas! as a
symbol of love overshadowed by uncertainty worse
than death.

Their home lay in the track of armies between the Rappahannock and the upper Potomac, and she with her young daughter had quitted it by night upon sudden warning of an advance of Union troops. Such a movement of the enemy would cut her off definitely from her husband and the son whom no love of hers could withhold from volunteering to fight in the Southern cause, and there had been brief delay in her decision to flit.

It had been dream-like at the time — how much more so after the lapse of years — that weird flitting from the safe, happy home whose foundations had seemed planted beyond the possibilities of change. The hurried packing — the hiding of valuables — the necessity of driving away at midnight down the familiar avenue, unknown to the sleeping black people — the meeting at daybreak with her husband, who had ridden north from his camp to welcome her — the feeling that all care was over, then. Next came the odd, helter-skelter, exciting life of refugees in war — the heart-beats and anguish of suspense in times of battle — the rapture of reunion with the spared. Both her husband and her beautiful eighteen-year old Hal had escaped without a scratch from almost continual fighting, when Lee in 1863 called upon his soldiers to follow him to Maryland. Hal, but recently promoted from the ranks to be a sergeant, had gone ahead without an opportunity to say good-by to his mother, then in Richmond.

"Don't fret, my darling; this means peace, home, everything," St. George Eustis had said when, recalled from his furlough to join the army on the march, he was aroused by his wife in the gray of morning. He had slept soundly while she had been long astir — setting last stitches, packing his portmanteau, brewing a cup of coffee, toasting bread. She had stood, before awakening her husband, watching him with her full soul in her gaze. "Think how we 've longed for this chance to push over the Potomac. I 'll get the shirts to Hal, and the stockings Una knit,—bless the dear baby, how she sleeps! . . . I 'm off now; keep a brave heart, Florence. God bless you both! Good-by."

He had stolen away on tiptoe to spare Una the pain of parting, but before his long strides had carried him the length of the corridor a little speeding form was on his track.

"Papa! I was not asleep. I tried to bear it, but I can't. Kiss me, my darling own papa!"

Eustis strained her to his heart. "Una, you will be brave? · You will think always of your mother first, and remember I trust her happiness to you?" These words rang in Una's ears long after the news came from Gettysburg that took the sunshine from her mother's life. When the tide of battle turned, and the last splendid assault of Pickett's Virginians was repulsed, Colonel Henry St. George Eustis was left for dead within the Federal lines. Those of his friends who saw him fall, quickly spread the tidings of their important loss. Farther down the slope, and farther down in the list of Confederate dead, was Hal Eustis, buried by his comrades near where he died. So much the mother learned beyond dispute, but of her husband nothing more than the fact of his fall beside a captured gun. Inquiries, letters, advertisements in the newspapers of both sides, failed to elicit further detail. As months wore on, she had let the conviction of his death sear its way into her soul. The shrinking of her means of livelihood cost her not a pang. Long practice as a volunteer nurse in the Confederate hospitals suggested to her a place as paid matron under Government, and to the hard routine of this employment she had come gladly. But for Una's comfort and well-being, the life of stern self-denial, of constant action in the ill-equipped camp, would have been her free choice. It was the rare moments of rest from labor Mrs. Eustis dreaded most.

Home visions thronged around the lonely little girl, bringing the hot tears of childhood to brim her eyes, but the sound of the door opening behind her made her spring quickly up, hiding her emotion by standing with her back to the amber glow.

"It's only me, Miss Una, darlin'," said Rose, one of two Irish sisters, laundry-maids who habited a room in the universal entry. She was a bright, hard-worked creature, and bore across her arms a spotless white frock of the thin stuff Una's mother liked best to see her wear.

"Rose! You have n't washed that, with all you have to do—and the day so very hot?"

"Whisht now, Miss Una, it's no credit to be washing where there ain't no dirt—an', if it's only to kape me hand in at clearstarchin' till this cruel war be's over. It'll go hard wid me sister an' me if we can't manage to do up our snowdrop's little frocks—not to speak of them beautiful gownds the madam was afther

givin' us a Chewsday — rale Frinch cambric with flowers like natur — it 's the sorrow that she can't be
wearin' 'em herself, and she wid a figgur like the
queen."

"Oh! She was beautiful, Rose, when you saw her
dressed in colors — but I must n't think of that! Look
how pretty our room is, Rose — but for the board
walls you 'd never believe it is in a hospital."

Busy Rose had but time to give an admiring glance
and hurry off, when a beloved visitor appeared, in the
shape of a lady whose autumnal charms were lightly
veiled in rice-powder, which, with the somewhat coquettish arrangement of her shabby dress, bespoke
that perennial charmer of the South, the belle of a
generation past.

"All alone, you dear little creature! Well, I did
hope to get a half-hour to myself, to come and sit
with you in this bower of beauty this afternoon; but
what between Doctor Snow and Major Isham, who
have this moment left me, and a poor fellow down
in ward 46 who 's to be operated on presently, and
will expect to see me around when the surgeons leave
— I 've brought you those sweet poems of L. E. L. to
read, my child, and a few Maryland biscuit for your
tea — wish with all my heart there were more of 'em,
but dear Mrs. Thompson's cook is famous for her
biscuit, and when this batch came to-day, I knew
there was many a poor soul — the sweetest verses, so
full of sentiment — I positively could n't get rid of
Isham — an old beau of mine, child, proposed to me
six times at the White Sulphur the year I became
engaged to poor Mr. Robbins — have n't seen him

since, and he vows I have n't changed a particle —
now, mind you come to me whenever I 'm off duty,
and your mama is on — give me a kiss to cheer me,
dear, for it 's ten to one that my pet patient will sink
after this amputation, and I must stay by him till he
goes."

"Take a bit of my geranium, dear Mrs. Robbins,"
cried Una, who knew by experience the tender un-
selfishness lurking under the shreds and patches of
this lady's vanity. "It will smell sweet to you in the
wards. And thank you a thousand times for the
biscuits. If you knew how I long for a home dainty,
now and again, that will tempt mama to eat."

She had not ceased to croon with satisfaction over
the unlooked-for bounty, when the one-armed and
one-legged soldier, employed to lower the headquarters flag at sunset, set flying upon the air a few very
wild echoes from the asthmatic bugle that was his
pride.

"There goes the flag to bed," cried Una, running
back to the window. "And now King David will be
here to take me out."

The rim of the sun had sunk behind the black
boles of the pine grove. Slowly the stars and bars
glided downward on their staff. Shortly thereafter
a shuffling step was heard outside Una's door, and a
deprecating tap upon its panels.

"*Come* in, King David," exclaimed the little lady,
insistently. "There is the trunk that I 've unpacked
now we 've a chest of drawers, and you 're to take it,
please, to the storeroom — that is, if you can carry it
by yourself."

"Light as a feather this is, honey," the old man said, stooping to deposit his torn straw hat upon the floor.

King David was an old negro, with a head too large for his body, and legs curiously bowed. When one spoke to him in kindness, his rugged face became irradiated with a smile pathetic in its humility; but there was dignity of the true royal sort in King David's bearing when one touched upon the honor of his master's house and family. He was the son of the old Mount Airy "Mammy," or head nurse (who had given him his name in sober tribute to the author of the Psalms), and had been, after the Southern fashion, apportioned to St. George Eustis in childhood as caretaker and general companion to the young heir of a great estate. Accompanying his mistress in her flitting to the Confederate lines, he had since clung to her shifting fortunes with increased fidelity. What it cost him to see his ladies reduced to their present condition of life, only those can understand who have personal acquaintance with the quality of old-time negro pride. He would have given his last morsel to save "My Mistis and little Mistis" from sitting down to break daily bread with some of the folk who shared their privileges. On this subject, Mrs. Eustis and he had to agree to differ.

"I, too, am a servant, David," she would say with a wan smile. "A paid servant of the Government, like you and all the rest."

"For the Lawd's sake, don't let anybody hear you say that, Mistis," he would whisper despairingly. "I don't reckon there's a soul in this camp that knows

you that ain't heard of the great family you came
from, and the way you 'n Marse Sainty gave your
money like water to start this war."

"Not a soul in the camp that knows *you*, David, I
dare say," she answered with a gleam of her old light
spirit.

To be near her and her child, King David had secured employment in the wards, and his pittance of
pay and rations was most often shared with those
poorer than himself. He had been a prayer leader of
renown in plantation days, and his missionary work
among the patients was generally more welcome than
the conventional ministrations of the Church. Early
and late he was seen at the bedside of the dying,
many of whom passed out of life clinging to his fingers
and repeating with fluttering breath his petition of
the sinner repenting at the gate of death.

It was the bright spot in King David's day when
sunset freed him to be at the disposal of his young
lady. The great heat during the day kept Una much
indoors, and she sorely missed the old out-door country life. To-day when King David had shouldered
her empty trunk and carried it away, she made haste
to take her shade-hat down from its peg, pausing
once more on the door-sill to look proudly back at
her final achievements in decoration.

"Is n't it *lovely*, King David," she said, when the
old man came twisting back. "Is n't this just like
a real home?"

"That it is, little Mistis," he answered cheerfully,
falling behind her, however, to gulp once or twice,
and swallow down a lump.

Hand-in-hand, homeless in a land of homes, the two wandered out of the precincts of the camp into a bowery bit of woodland overhanging a canal that here kept sluggish pace with the river tumbling below over its rocky bed. The sweet untainted air was balmy with wild flowers. Una, soon tired of walking, sat upon the root of a tree looking down into the clear stream, drawing long breaths of the delicious atmosphere, trying to forget the sad scenes and to deaden her ears to the haunting sounds of Camp Winder life. As she rested thus, a canal-boat glided beneath her, a negro boy, stretched on the deck, performing upon the horn an obligato of rare melody, which died in the distance like the horns of Elfland. And then a bird in the tree-top overhead took up the tale of sweetness, trilling in ecstasy as if there were no war.

"Oh! King David," said the little girl, "do you know, what with the furniture and this lovely evening, I think if it were not wrong I could be almost happy?"

"Whatever you do, don't stop feelin' good when you _kin_, little Mistis," he replied, standing beside her leaning upon his staff. "It's nature movin' in your veins like the sap stirs in the trees. You've got to do a mighty heap of laughin' to put heart into your pore ma, honey, don't forgit."

"I know it. I like to make her face soften and her lips curve. King David, I believe she has never given up hope that my father may be alive."

"It's nigh onto a year, now, Miss Una," he said reluctantly, stooping down to pick a bunch of wood anemones that he might hide his face. His mind's

eye saw his beloved master on a veritable throne of
glory side by side with Master Hal, both playing
golden harps.

Una's face clouded, and she sighed heavily.

"We will walk on now, King David. I must gather
some wild flowers for her little Sèvres vase. She will
come in tired, I know. Oh! One can't have everything, but Mrs. Robbins gave me some such beautiful biscuits, and I *could* manage to get a little butter
—if we *only* had a pinch of real tea."

If King David had carried the wealth of the Indies
in his pocket, he could not have broken into a more
widely jubilant smile.

"Miss Una, honey, sure as you 're born, I 've got a
s'prise for you. You dun hit the nail square on the
head that time, my lamb. Ef I didn't scrub her store-
room flo' for Miss Potts after hours last night, and
she give me my choice of pay, 'tween a ham-bone and
a drawin' o' tea — the gynnwine article, her nephew
sent her a pound of through the blockade! I reckon
I tuk the tea. I was projeckin' to keep it till next
time Mistis has one of her headaches."

"Oh! that is too good!" cried Una, her face kind-
ling. It did not occur to her to thank him, so identi-
cal were their interests. "I 'm afraid she 's had too
many headaches lately, and I think her step is slower
than it was — if it was n't that she has always had
good health —"

"She ain't lookin' so mighty well, honey," the old
man admitted, then stopped. He had not the heart
to cloud the child's holiday hour with a fear that had
begun to haunt him.

15

Una walked home wreathed like a Dryad with her
wild flowers, and in passing through the gangrene
tents flitted in here and there to lay some vine or
spray upon the pillows of sufferers condemned to
that dreaded exile from the world. A little cluster
of anemones, with rose and purple staining milk
white petals, alone remained to deck the tea-table improvised from Miss Sprigg's rosewood bedstand, at
which, presiding over a plate of biscuits toasted and
buttered, Una received her mother — King David
bowing behind her with a pot of smoking tea.

Mrs. Eustis tried to respond to the old man's pride,
the little girl's delight. She drank eagerly a cup of
tea, but ate a morsel only, and sat by the window,
courting the faint stirring of the close air at night-
fall, conscious of a strange weakness and swimming
of the head. The latter hours of her weary day had
been spent with a patient who had begged her for his
mother's sake to stay by him, until, just as the lights
of the camp were flickering feebly forth, his lamp of
life went out. Until long after bedtime she lay upon
the lounge undressed, and by the next morning was
declared by the doctors to be in the first stage of a
malarial fever, its exact nature not yet assured.

Una, who had never seen her mother ill, felt a sense
of terror overmaster her solicitude. With a sinking
heart she set about making her dear invalid comfortable. Irish Rose, coming in and seeing Mrs. Eustis
toss upon the harsh, unbleached cotton of the hospital
sheets, hastened away to extract from the bottom of
her old-fashioned chest an armful of snowy linen.

"Let me put these on her bed, me burd," the good

creature whispered. "Ra'al old-country flax it is,
spun and wove by me mother, God rist her sowl; and
the lace on the pilly-cases she worked and bid me put
by against me weddin'-day; though the saints above
knows whin I 'll get a chance at a husband, seein' the
way the Yankees be's a shortnin' our supply of min-
folks.

Mrs. Robbins and King David shared Una's vigil,
as hour by hour, day by day, the fever ran its course.
One night, following a day when the sound of guns
had ceased only as the darkness came, the little
girl had fallen asleep on the lounge, while King
David kept watch over the sufferer. Toward morning a tap was heard upon their door, and the ward-
master of a newly equipped ward in Mrs. Eustis's
division asked, in a low tone, for permission to use
the matron's keys.

"There 's an ambulance train just beginning to
come in, and all my beds will be full," the man said
to Una, who answered his appeal. "The most of 'em
have n't had food since before the fight this morning,
and if you *could* make it convenient, Miss, to come
out to the store-room and show me where things are
kept, it would save time and life too."

"Go, Una darling," said her mother. "Do for me
what I cannot do. You know where I keep the brandy
—make it go far, for it is all we have—never fear,
but David will take good care of this poor soldier
fallen at her post."

Lantern in hand the man strode ahead of her as
Una under the starlight picked her way across the
rough soil of the camp to the ward-kitchen where

they hastily reviewed supplies. To her dismay, not a
mouthful of food was available, except a few "pones"
of coarse corn-bread, a little cold boiled bacon and a
couple of quarts of milk.

"How many to feed, Henderson?" she asked mourn-
fully.

"God knows, Miss, but considerable more'n we've
got food to give 'em, I'm afraid. Will you take the
bottle and a cup, Miss? There'll be some too far gone
to eat, better's the luck for them."

The Southern night had spent its early heat, and a
delicious breeze laden with wood odors came up from
the river. In the blue vault of heaven great stars
shone brilliantly. On the confines of the camp, before the open doors of the new ward, ambulances
were depositing their ghastly burdens, some of the
wounded uttering pitiful prayers to be left to die in
peace, some mercifully in stupor, while other forms
were lifted out frozen in the silence of eternal rest.
Those for whom the long, jolting ride through heat
and dust from the battlefield had not finished the
work begun by the enemy's bullets were carried within
and laid upon cots in rows, and by the insufficient
glimmer of oil-lamps and tallow dips the surgeons
began their rounds. Una, too inured to these scenes
of sorrow to lose her balance, set to work immediately
to count the men requiring sustenance, and to divide
her scant supplies. With the ward-helpers, she went
from bed to bed distributing the bread and meat to a
few, to more the eagerly craved draught of milk which
must be doled out in such tantalizing measure. Here
and there, at the surgeon's orders, she parted with

the brandy that was as precious as the elixir of life.
Despite her calm, tears of bitter longing for more
milk ran down her cheeks and mingled with the
cup she had forcibly to withdraw from parched and
starving lips.

Almost the last sufferer upon her round was a
young fellow who had worked himself over upon his
face and lay without sign of life. Una looked about
for help to move him, but no one was at leisure and,
slipping her soft hand under his cheek, she turned it
to the light, striving with the other hand to put a
spoonful of milk and brandy between his white lips.
Then a cry burst from the little girl, unheeded in the
commotion of the hour.

"Denny! Denny Ryan! Speak to me. Drink this
for my sake; for Hal's sake, Denny, only hear."

A surgeon, attended by an orderly carrying a lantern, hurried up. The light fell full upon the wounded
lad, upon Una's imploring face.

"Oh! Doctor Lewis, help him, *please*," she said.
" He was one of my father's soldiers and followed my
brother to the war. He lived on our place, and we've
been playmates all my life."

"He is past helping, my dear child," the doctor
answered kindly. "You may stay by him, if you like,
and if consciousness returns, your voice will soothe
him, but he is going fast."

"That's a pocket edition of Florence Nightingale
you've got there, doctor," said a newly transferred
assistant on the staff, as they resumed work at an adjoining bed.

· "She is one of the precious things that come in

small parcels," answered Lewis. "Such pluck and sweetness don't meet every day."

Una knelt by Denny's side, weeping silently. The sight of his familiar freckled face brought back a hundred visions of home and Hal and her father. Denny, the son of the Mount Airy Irish overseer, had been Hal's loyal shadow; had refused to stay behind him from the war, had been with him at his death at Gettysburg. Ryan, Denny's father, had, so far as the widow and daughter of Colonel Eustis knew, remained on at Mount Airy in charge of their property—his older son Bill having gone off to Washington and enlisted as a Federal volunteer. And this was the end of poor Denny's soldiering. So soon to follow Hal. Always to follow Hal. Above the bed was a window, through which the streaks of a saffron dawn came to blend with the shadows of the ward. In a tree near by, a bird began to stir and chirp. The boy opened his eyes and looked at his companion wondering.

"Miss Una! I thought you was calling me. It was picking dewberries, I was—down in the cow-pasture where the blue flags grows—at home."

"Dear Denny, you are not at home yet, but you soon will be. Don't you remember you were in a fight to-day, and they 've brought you straight to me, at Camp Winder where we 've lived since—papa and Hal were—left at Gettysburg."

"*Hurrah! We charged the ridge!*" Denny cried out in a thrilling pipe that caused more than one head to turn on its weary pillow. "Miss Una, I 'd 'a' died to bring Hal safe out of it. To take him and

leave me was kind o' funny, don't you think? Miss
Una, did Bill tell you he saw the Colonel in the
Yankee hospittle?"

Una's heart gave a great, eager leap that robbed
her of her speech. To Denny "the Colonel" was
always Una's father.

"Hal and I are goin' trappin' Molly cottontails ·
to-morrow," the voice went on more feebly. "In the
wood where we got you the mistletoe last Christmas —
it's snowin' now, I think — my han's are gittin' cold."

Una took his chill fingers in her warm clasp, and
summoned all her strength.

"Denny," she said close in his dying ear, "for
God's sake try to understand. *Tell me what Bill said
about papa.*"

"Miss Una, was you talkin'? Seems to me I'm a
little deef."

"What did Bill say about the Colonel in the
hospital?"

"It was last Monday — on picket-guard near Drewry's Bluff — I saw Bill an' hailed him. You bet he
was surprised. . . . We talked back an' fort' a good
half-hour. Bill said the Colonel was n't killed at
all . . . he was just a bit childish-like, an' couldn't
talk . . . Miss Una, are you cryin' for your pa?"

"Denny —"

"Bill's a good fellow, mother. He'll fetch the
cows, i'stead of me. . . . Hold on there, Hal, I'm
comin." . . .

And with that, poor Denny died.

## II

Was it true — this wonderful news that poor Denny's fevered brain had schooled his stammering tongue to utter? Dared she believe that their beloved one was not indeed left "free among the dead" on the heights at Gettysburg? Wings to her feet carried Una over the rude pathways of the camp back to the barracks where, in their poor room, her ailing mother lay.

There sat King David at his post beside the bed, unwearied, motionless, his face stern and rigid like a mask of gray marble. He had pinned over the shadeless window a worn old shawl, and it was quite dark in the room except where a thread of morning light came through a moth-hole and slanted across the invalid's pillow. She was sleeping an unrestful sleep, and in her cheeks burned crimson spots, but Una thought she had never seen the beautiful clear-cut features stand out in such relief from their surroundings — the look of race so prominent.

"King David, is she worse?"

"Nothing you mout' n't have expected, honey. The doctor he kem in 'bout four o'clock, an' tole us where you was, an' she sez then she was n't sufferin' much, an' she was glad her little girl was doin' her work for her. Miss Robbins and Miss Rose has been back an' fort.' Hes it been a tryin' night for you, my honey?"

"Oh! King David, don't talk about me now. I have heard such a wonderful thing that I believe my heart will burst unless I tell you. Shall we disturb mama by talking?"

"No, chile; the fever's dun took a holt of her too hard for that. 'Fore you tries to talk, tho', honey, I've got bread and coffee for you, I begged Miss Rose to git me. The coffee's cold, I reckon, but you must drink it, an' set you down on this cheer an' rest awhile. You'll need to be strong before she wakes again, Miss Una. She's off her head consid'able."

At this moment the sufferer stirred, opened wide her unconscious eyes, and spoke in quick, excited tones:

"Go, mammy. Hurry and tell your master. He'll be so glad the baby is a girl. Does Hal know about his sister? How I long to see them side by side."

She fashioned her bedclothes into a little roll, and pressed it to her bosom. Then, dashing it away, she threw her white arms high above her head, and cried out in a thrilling voice:

"God has smitten me to the earth. By night, by day, I cry to Him for my husband and my son, but He is deaf. His face is turned from me. I am bereaved, I am bereaved."

Una burst into a passion of tears. Starting forward, she tried to imprison her mother's form in her arms, but was cast aside like a broken reed. Taking Mrs. Eustis in his powerful grasp, soothing her with tenderest murmurs, the old negro held his mistress on her pillow; and when, calmed and controlled, she passed into another interval of sleep, he stooped and picked the little sobbing creature from the floor, where she had fallen in a heap.

"It's hard for you, my lamb, the first time you've ever seen her out 'n her head. But don't you be

afeard, my blessin'. This here fever 's got to run its
course, the doctor says. It makes my heart ache to
see her thinkin' she 's home again. The Lawd's will
be done, honey; but ef thar 's anything I do begrutch
my enemies, it 's the Chamber at Mount Airy. I 've
been sittin' here all night, chile, thinkin' 'bout your
pore ma's fo'-pos' bed, an' them dimity curtains with
the drop fringe, as your blessed gran'ma made.
There, there! stop cryin', my baby. Your ma 'll
git well; she 's got the gyniwine Stuart constitoo-
tion. Why, you 're laughin', Miss Una! Save us
and bless us, ef the chile ain't got high-strikes!"

"Oh! you don't know, King David," the little girl
said, choking down her tears. "You don't understand. It is n't only about mama. Oh! let me cry
a minute longer, and I shall be able to tell you the
wonderful news I 've heard. The doctor told you
it was poor Denny I stayed with till he died. But he
did n't tell you, King David — see, I am quiet now,
and you may trust me — what Denny said with his
last breath. Denny saw Bill on picket-guard, near
Drewry's Bluff, and Bill told him — oh! my heart will
break with joy — told him my father was n't killed.
Bill saw him in a hospital — *saw papa*, King David!"

The old negro's face worked with powerful emotion. A dry sob burst from him, and, straightway
falling on his knees, he raised his hands to Heaven.

"If this be true, Oh! Lawd most marciful!" he
prayed, "then hear thy sarvant now. Hast thou
not said that them whom Gawd has j'ined together,
let no man put asunder? Bring back to thy hand-
maiden the husband of her youth. Lift up her

stricken head and wipe her tears away. Renew her
in love, in wealth, in happiness, and sanctify us
and her unto thy sarvice, for thy dear Son's sake.
Amen!"

"Sainty, my darling," came from the tossing figure
on the bed, "put your arms around me. Hold me
close. There, I can rest now. Hold me close."

.     .     .     .     .     .

NEVER before, in the course of their companion-
ship, had the grizzled old head and the sunny young
one been called on to do such an amount of indepen-
dent thinking, now that the brain that had judged
for them was clogged, and the hand that had steered
their course was nerveless. The two found time
to steal away from the sick room to walk behind
Denny's rough coffin to Hollywood and see it laid
upon another like it in a soldiers' trench. Una's
hands showered pink azaleas from the woods into
the double grave, and King David, kneeling upon
the ground "undone" by many a yawning pit half
filled with water, prayed long and fervently.

"Come, uncle," said one of the men, touching him
on the shoulder. "I reckon it's 'bout time for you to
be dryin' up. There's another cart-load waitin' to be
tucked away, an' we ain't got time to do this thing in
style."

Died for his country! Thus Denny Ryan and
many another like him came to a patriot's reward!

Yes, the fever must run its course; and day after
day Mrs. Eustis turned on her hard bed, where noises
racked her tortured brain, where burning heat drank

all freshness from the air, where noisome smells arose
from the trenches around the camp, where, worse
than all, a plague of insects issued from the pine
walls and overran their quarters. People were kind,
and from the wards, where Una tried to take her
mother's place, came many a message of love and
gratitude, while their fellow-workers, high and lowly,
vied with each other in striving to ease the burden
that little Una bore so patiently. But the time came
when Dr. Lewis saw that, to recover, his patient must
breathe another atmosphere. Faithful Miss Sprigg,
from her retreat in the country, wrote to offer an asylum to Mrs. Eustis, whom they had not ventured to
tell of Denny Ryan's news, in a farm-house far away
from the town. But Miss Sprigg was very poor, and
it was as much as her kind friends could do to take
in one other inmate to their crowded home. Una
must remain in the charge of Mrs. Robbins and King
David at the hospital.

Una heard this decision with a beating heart. Hard
as it was, it gave her courage to unfold to Dr. Lewis
a scheme that had been evolved during many consul-
tations between King David and herself.

"You are sure my mother is out of danger, Dr.
Lewis?" she asked their kind physician, who had
quite taken this "brave baby" to his heart.

"She will have every chance now in her favor.
The change of air should work marvels. If it were
not for the extraordinary lassitude—her strong
nerves seem to have gone all to pieces suddenly;
but you need have no fear at being separated from
her for a while. She recognizes the inevitable, and

bows to it. When she comes back to us, my dear, I
hope you will both forget this present trial, as nobly
as you have lived down all the rest."

Una saw her mother driven away in an ambulance
lent by Government to its servant fallen by the way,
and then turned and resolutely faced her friends, a
new light shining in her eyes.

"There is but one thing that will make her well,
Dr. Lewis, and you and Mrs. Robbins must help me
to work it out. I mean to keep my promise to my
father, and give her back to him."

.     .     .     .     .     .

"THAT little sprite!" pondered the doctor to himself. "And that simple-minded old darky, who was
never off a plantation in his life till now! The idea
seems preposterous. And yet, stranger things have
been accomplished; there 's a chance. In time of
war we catch at straws. Una will win her way where
a battalion might fall back. God bless her! I 'll help
her all I can."

Their plan was to journey into the Valley, and
there make their way as best they could through
the debatable ground harried by frequent fightings,
to Mount Airy, where, from Denny's father, the lost
clue might be taken up. Means for the journey
were secured by the eager sacrifice of Una's string
of pearls, an heirloom put aside against her time of
appearance in society. The few clothes she ventured
to take were packed in a portmanteau by Mrs. Robbins, Rose and Bridget, who showered upon their
task many a fervent tear and blessing. King

16

David's equipment for the enterprise consisted of a parcel so flat and spare that the Doctor laughed when he inquired if the old man meant to carry into the Northern lines only the supposed uniform of a Georgia major—a shirt-collar and a pair of spurs.

"And ef I were just takin' a clean bandanna an' a couple o' biled collars along, sir," said David, with a show of wounded feeling, "it was in no ways my purpose to discredit my little mistis o' Sundays, on the road. There's always cricks and runs, sir, where I kin do my washin' overnight, an' I need my hands to carry her carpet-bag."

"All right, old fellow, of course you do. It was only my little joke," the surgeon hastened to say, pressing a roll of Confederate bluebacks into his hand. "Put this into your pipe and smoke it on the way. And mind—but I need n't tell you this—to keep watch over your Miss Una day and night."

"Sarvant, sir, much obleeged to you," answered the old darky, bowing like a prince. "You won't have any call to be disapp'inted in them particulars with me. The Lawd do so with me and mine ef I ain't worthy of this trus'."

Dr. Lewis saw the travelers off on the train for Lynchburg, and turned back with a tightening in his throat.

"It 's womankind like that, that make the true sinews of war, I 'm thinking," muttered he in his black beard.

A day later the travelers set forth on the first stage of their haphazard journey through a region where all ordinary methods of conveyance had been

interrupted by war. It was an earthly paradise, that
fertile vale, dominated by the grand Peaks of Otter
or watered by Shenandoah, "Daughter of the Stars."
But a few weeks earlier, Sigel's boys in blue had
marched merrily along those green defiles to find their
way blocked by Breckenridge, his depleted ranks of
veterans eked out with lads from the Military Academy at Lexington, whose gallant fight has gone into
history among the famous achievements of the time.
At Piedmont, again, the "rebs" were put to rout, their
leader killed. And so the pendulum went on vibrat-
ing in those days of early June.

Una found herself in the rear of a hooded cart
drawn by mules, sitting amid crates that had held
poultry, the space in front filled up by King David
and the driver—a farmer returning from the nearest
town, where he had been to sell his feathered live-
stock at a sacrifice to avoid having them "pressed"
by stragglers from either of the armies. It was slow
progress; but the child, whose eyes had rested for so
long upon rows of wards and tents, and grass trodden
into a clay soil, gazed from the aperture at the back
enchanted. What to her were fallen fences, fields
trampled by cavalry, burned houses, when above rose
those sapphire summits melting into the vast azure of
a sky in June? When the mules splashed aside into a
shallow, limpid stream, and dipped their noses in for
a long and rapturous drink, King David scrambled
out and brought her a bunch of calycanthus shrubs,
with a leaf-cup full of currants from the garden of a
desolated farm-house by the road. Trifles like this,
with the music of wayside brooks, the carol of birds,

the shifting of cloud-prints on the mountain-sides,
made variety enough to wile away the long hours of
plodding.   Tired out at last, toward evening she fell
asleep on a bundle of hay in the bottom of the cart,
nor stirred till the stopping of their wheels showed
that they had arrived at a dwelling dimly indicated
by a light streaming upon darkness, and the loud
barking of a dog.

"Wake up, my honey; you must ask the lady of
the house — ra'al purty, the purtiest you can — to let
you stop here to-night."

Una could not know that the faint-hearted quaver
in King David's voice, and the total withdrawal of
farmer Lucas from participation in the affair, were
due to their wholesome fear of the farmer's shrewish
wife.   They had come to a halt before a threshold
within which stood, clad in domestic cotton, lamp in
hand, a gaunt figure sending forth upon the night
the querulous utterings of a woman who casts about
her for a wrong; and Una, half awake, was urged
forward by the men to stand where the light fell
upon her upturned, pleading face.   With the quaint
courtesy habitual to her, she told her tale and proffered her request.

"Well, you do be a mite to be travelin' around
like this, an' nuthin' but that old nigger-man to look
out for you.   Long 's you 're here, got to take you
in, I reckon; but that nigger 's got to march out to
the barn, double-quick.   Sick an' tired am I of lodgin' strangers, an' bein' eat out o' house an' home;
an' Mr. Lucas knows it well enough."

Mr. Lucas, in the shadow of the cart, bestowed

upon King David a jovial nudge to signify that mat-
ters had taken a satisfactory turn; and the men disappeared together in the friendly darkness, while
Una followed her guide into the house. Here, although the complaining voice ceased not to find
fault with everything, the guest, ensconced in an
arm-chair, was served, from a flowered plate and cup,
with crisp johnny-cake and milk. A cat nestling to
her knee and finally jumping into her lap to wreathe
its tail across her neck, completed her sense of comfort. And when her sleepy yellow head nodded
upon her breast, a pair of long, thin arms that were
certainly not David's swooped down and bore the
little traveler to bed.

Late in the night, a sound as of thunder broke
Una's sleep. She sat up in her bed beneath the
roof-peak and awoke gradually, to hear the tramp-
ling of horses around the house. Voices hailed the
slumberers within, a knock resounding upon the
door. Then, over the tumult, arose a familiar sound
—the scolding of Mrs. Lucas. The remonstrant
tones of the farmer appealed at intervals, in vain.
When at last the door opened, and the master of the
house, in shirt and trousers, issued desperately forth,
a torrent of fresh invective followed him.

"Blamed if I had n't rather sleep on your hay, old
man, than face that battery inside," said a hearty voice.
"But we 're obliged to ask you for a sup and bite.
We 're Cornfeds, and blasted hungry ones at that."

"Cornfeds or Yanks, it 's all one to me," was the
reply from behind the door. "It 'll be like as if the
seventeen-year locusts had passed over this place."

But the soldiers had their way, and the little house soon shook with their tread, while talk and laughter, tobacco-smoke and the clank of accoutrements came up the narrow stair to Una's ear. When she had heard the men divide forces, one half to sleep on the hay in the barn beside the horses, the rest to sprawl as they could on the floor of the living-room below, the child went back smiling to her nest, nor stirred till next morning's light brought the apparition of the farmer's wife to mingle with some dream that her mother's fingers had been toying with her hair.

"Come, git up now," Mrs. Lucas said sharply, emptying a pail of clean water into a tub at her bedside. "There 's soap and a towel on the cheer, and I 've shuck out your things. Soon as you 's ready, you kin come down and git a mouthful o' breakfast I saved after them consarned critters had clar'd out. Would n't have had an aig to bless myself if I had n't locked up my two best hens in the cupboard with the old man's Sunday clo'es."

"Oh! have the soldiers gone?" cried Una, in disappointment.

"Yes, thank goodness, all but two on 'em, and they 'd be sleepin' yet, but I broomed 'em off the floor with a mop and a pail o' water."

"How good you are to give me this nice bath, and to get my clothes so clean," the child said gratefully, sitting up in bed, and letting all her bright hair loose like a glory around her face. "It 's just what my own mother would have done. It seems such a pity you have n't any little girl to love and take care of."

The woman looked at her for a moment with a curiously softened gaze; then, with her mouth twitching, went over to a chest in the corner and took out a child's frock and sunbonnet of faded pink calico, smelling of lavender.

"Them was my gal's," she said briefly. "Died o' scarlet fever 'bout your age. Hed hair like corn-silk, jest like yours. Come now, up with you, and dress yourself. Hain't time to dawdle here, and all my work a-waitin' to be done." And, whirling out of the room, she shut the door with a vicious snap.

Una slipped down, to find a meal laid for her below. The room was in spotless order, and empty but for her friend the cat; but on the door-stone outside sat a couple of gray-shirted soldiers, smoking corn-cob pipes in the cool shadow of a lilac-bush in bloom; David, in the road beyond, held their horses, champing to be off. At sight of the child, refreshed by sleep and dewy from her bath, the men pulled themselves together, and one of them, a huge fellow with a boy's face, gazed with open-mouthed admiration. The other, a lieutenant in command of the body of scouts that had gone on ahead, spoke to her courteously.

"I 've been hearing about your trip from uncle, here," he said, "and I wish K Company could help you along the way, Miss. But just now, unless we 're turned back, we 're going in the opposite direction from Glenmont where you 're bound. Road 's pretty free from Yanks; that 's one comfort; and I 've told the old man the best way to go."

"Oh! thank you," said Una, fervently. "If you

knew how sound it made me sleep when I heard our
dear soldiers ride up here last night!"

But the colloquy was interrupted by Mrs. Lucas,
who, frying-pan in hand, issued from the door, and
demanded to know if "them *calvary* was a-goin' to
block up her front door all day?" at which a general
shrinkage of spirit ensued among the men-folk in
hearing of her voice, and the troopers hastily sprang
into their stirrups and galloped off, singing mock-
ingly:

> "If you want to have a good time,
> Jine the *calvary*, jine the *calvary*."

"We has to foot it a good piece to-day, my honey,"
said King David, when the travelers, having paid
their bill, set out, under fire of a tornado of abuse
of him because of a muddy footprint he left on the
floor on meekly entering to take Una's bag in hand.

"I wish she had said good-by," said Una, distress-
fully. "See here, King David, as she almost pushed
me out, she put in my hand this nice parcel of lunch.
I think she's the strangest woman I ever saw, but she
must be really good *at heart*, don't you think so?"

Thus cornered, David scratched his head. They
were under shelter of the hen-house, and compara-
tively safe. Drawing a long breath, he said in the
discreetest of whispers:

"It ain't the first time the good Lawd has made
honey to come out of a cur'us place, chile. The car-
cass of the lion brought fo'th sweetness. Gawd moves
in a mysterious way, his wonders to perfo'm."

Past blossoming hedge-rows, past orchard and

meadow fragrant with smells of June, into an arch-
ing wood-road as the sun climbed higher. Una
thought there could be no method of travel so much
to her taste. Their destination was the house of a
farmer from whom it was likely they could hire a
horse and cart to forward them on their way. But
when, just as the child's strength and spirit began to
flag, and they came at noontide out of the cross-cut
through the woods upon the clearing to which they
had been directed, a direful disappointment greeted
them. House and outbuildings there were none;
only a series of charred spots remained in the middle
of a trampled and desolated field of growing corn.

"It 's a fresh fire—smokin' yit," said King David.
"Lawd help the pore folks as was driv' away from
here."

While the two stood disconsolate, a clatter of hoofs
was heard in a bit of woods beyond.

"It 's cavalry, honey," said King David, breath-
lessly. "Let 's git in hidin' behind that clump o'
sumacs yonder. They 'll never look to see us here."

Before Una had time to realize her fear, the soldiers were upon them, and, identifying the party of
Confederates who had slept overnight at the Lucas
farm, King David waved his old hat with a rousing
cheer.

"Hello, old tarrypin, did n't expect to see us again
so soon," called out their leader, coming to a halt.
"Well, boys, this is the place we 're to wait for the
lieutenant, and if I 'm not mistaken, there 's a good
spring at the end of the path behind that watermelon
patch."

In a trice the horses were unsaddled and tethered in the wood. Canteens were filled at the spring, rations were produced, and the bivouac began.

From the trunk of a fallen tree, where Una sat to eat her luncheon, while King David knelt brushing her dusty boots, she looked over affectionately at the ring of troopers lolling like Olympian gods at ease. Presently a couple of horsemen came galloping out of the glade, and she recognized with delight her friends of the morning.

"Well, Miss, we 've met again sooner than we thought," said the lieutenant. "This is a bad business for poor farmer Gray. We heard down below that he 'd been raided last night, and it seems the family 's cleared out for parts unknown. The nearest place for you to sleep to-night is Glenmont, ten miles off, and it 's past me how you 're goin' to get there in this heat. We 've got a pair of extra nags since yesterday, and if you can manage to sit on a man's saddle, Miss, we 'll mount you, after dark, when we move on. I s'pose you can stick to a bareback colt, old man, eh?"

"I reckon thar ain't much hoss-flesh that can better me, sir," said David, his eyes shining with delight at the unlooked-for help. "An' I 'm beholden to you more than I can say, for givin' a lift to my little mistis."

As Una's story found its way to the ears of the curious troopers, there was not a man among them who did not mentally constitute himself her protector and devotee. But when, at dark, she was lifted up to sit behind the peak of a cavalry-saddle, where she kept to her slippery perch with an ease born of early habit, she found at her bridle-rein John Britton, the big lumbering fellow who had been the comrade of the lieutenant at the farm. King David, astride of a frisky filly who till that morning had been at large in comfortable pastures, had as much as he could do to keep the wilful creature's back. Una's huge knight held along with her, saying little, but watching every movement of her horse, while before, behind and on the other side rode her stalwart body-guard. Forward in dead silence, making little noise on the soft wood road, listening to every rustle of the leaves, passed the ghostly cavalcade, under the light of stars, amid the chirp of the frogs, the chant of whippoorwills.

In thick darkness. A little hamlet with shutters obstinately closed, behind which lights glimmered like eyes watching through half-shut lids. At the first stroke of horses' hoofs upon the narrow street, some of the lights went out, keys and bolts were heard to creak in their wards. One could almost count the heart-beats of the anxious folk inside. Then a sergeant, who could whistle like a bird, uttered a bar or two of "The Bonnie Blue Flag," and, at once, open flew doors and windows, out trooped the villagers, offering food and shelter for man and beast.

Una, taken into the home and tucked under the diamond-patterned quilt of a good old dressmaker, slept deliciously till dawn, when it was agreed by her friend the lieutenant that she should again resume the march with him under the conditions of the night before. The old woman cried over her as she brought out a feather pillow for a saddle-pad,

and tucked a bagful of biscuits and cookies into the
child's lap. Una herself had no thought of tears as
she rode triumphantly away. She knew that every
movement forward brought her nearer her precious
goal. The troopers, won more and more by her
modest acceptance of their comradeship, treated her
like a little wandering queen assigned to their special charge. But it was to big John Britton, known
familiarly to them as "Baby Mine," the others tacitly
awarded the right of attendance at her bridle-rein.
When they reached the river ford, he stretched forth
a mighty arm to lift her like a thistle-down upon his
horse's neck, and, plunging in, they buffeted the noisy
yellow current gallantly. Una's cheeks bloomed and
her eyes sparkled as their horse emerged dripping
and snorting with excitement, first to gain a foothold
upon the slippery far bank. Then, as the day wore
on, how sweet the odor of the woods, the shady bivouac to lunch upon soldier's fare! And the joy of
the long bright afternoon, broken by mysterious ap-
pearances ahead of scouts to proclaim the way secure!
She watched almost grudgingly the day decline that
was to be her last of such congenial fellowship.

"Well, I reckon the best of friends must part,"
said the lieutenant, when in the evening they put her
with her old man down at a roadside house. He
made an attempt to be jocular, but his keen eyes
showed his sympathy with the waifs thus set adrift.

Una, in her confiding way, went the rounds of her
body-guard, shaking hands with each, and standing
on tiptoe, last of all, to leave a kiss and a tear between
the eyes of her good gray steed.

"Oh! I shall never, never forget you," she said with a pathetic break in her voice as she stood facing them. "And when I see papa I shall tell him how soldiers helped a soldier's daughter. Good-by, good-by, dear friends, and thank you a thousand times."

Last to take leave of her was "Baby Mine." He had a sheepish look upon his sunburned face, and as Una offered him her hand with a graciously tender smile, he bowed low as if he meant to press his lips to it, then, blushing scarlet, desisted and turned awkwardly away. In her clasp, however, he left a crumpled leaf from a soldier's pocket-book, on which, when they were out of sight, Una read these penciled words:

Wen yo mete yore pa, tell him yo have maid a bad man pray that he may git yo safe, an' I am yore frend til deth.

JOHN BRITTON,
—— Co., —— Regt., Va. Cavlry.

### III

"KEEP your sperets up, my baby," said King David, forcing a cheerful note. "They's boun' to be a house somewheres along here."

It was the close of their third day afoot. In the dusty highway, under the vertical beams of a summer sun, Una had walked, until a happy cross-cut through field and forest had cooled her sore feet in verdure; but now her white cheeks and flagging steps told the tale of her fatigue. They had wasted time and strength in losing their way in this region denuded

17

of ordinary landmarks by the war-cyclone. The better class of houses they had passed were mostly vacant. The cabins where disheartened poor whites and negroes still lingered were a sorry refuge. They had gone hungry for miles to-day; and now upon the horizon King David's eager eye beheld no sign of human habitation.

"Don't you think we might camp here in the woods, King David?" she asked, breaking her patient silence. "Anything would be better than the house we slept in last night."

"My little mistis sha'n't sleep on the ground if I can holp it," the negro answered in the most lively tones at his command. Inside, the heart of him was lead. He saw violet shadows coming upon the pearl of her cheeks; and at the foot of the next rise of the road she stopped and panted.

"Honey lamb, you 're not a-goin' to faint?" he cried. Una did not speak, but smiled at him after a wan fashion. Picking her up in his arms, the old man went a few paces up the hill and scoured the region ahead of him with his gaze. A little way before, he saw the gable of a house, with what he took to be a lamp shining out of its casement.

"Glory Hallelujah!" he exclaimed. "Ef thar ain't some Christian soul that lit her lamp to be a light unto our feet. Now, little Miss, you just keep quiet and let me carry you."

Una could not remonstrate, so spent were her forces. She lay very still as he toiled upward, keeping her eyes fixed upon the heaven above.

"King David."

"What say, chile ?"

"Do you remember that picture of a young man,
over the sideboard in the Mount Airy dining-room?"

"Sartin I does, Miss Una. He was one o' them
graneestors of your pa's in England, I 've heard tell.
A powerful sot-lookin' young gentleman."

"All our lives, Hal and I have wanted to have a
chance to do something like what he did. Something that never seemed likely to happen in our
quiet country lives."

"En what did the gentleman do, honey? 'Pears
like I 've heard, but I kind o' disremember."

Thus cunning David tried to wile her into forget-
fulness of the stress of this hour that filled his own
heart with aching.

"He was a young soldier, King David, and he
lived about two hundred years ago. He was sent on
a journey full of danger, to carry a message that
would help to restore a king to his rightful throne.
It was a journey a little like ours, King David, in a
country where soldiers were roaming around on
horseback — moss-troopers they were called. . . .
Hal and I often played 'Sir Lionel.' Hal always
wanted to be *it*, you know, but he said I could n't be
fierce enough for the robber, and so I was generally
Sir Lionel. . . . Are you listening, King David?"

"Sure I is, Miss Una."

"The real Sir Lionel had to go in winter, and that
was far worse than ours. He wrote that story about
it in the yellow old paper papa keeps in the secretary
in his study. . . . He rode on and on over hill
and dale, 'where the moonshine and the snow made

the nights as clear as day.' I always remember
that. . . . 'Iter Boreale,' he called it . . . that
means a northern journey, King David . . . I never
thought I should take a real northern journey without Hal. . . ."

"Miss Una, is you mindin' what I told you about
keepin' your sperets up,—for your mother's and
father's sakes, my dear?"

"Of course I mind; . . . the only trouble I have
is that I am so heavy for you to carry."

"No mor' 'n a snow-bird on a cedar twig, my honey.
Can't you tell me some more about your pa's brave
grancestor?"

"One night, in the dale country, Sir Lionel was set
upon by a notorious robber, with whom he had a
fierce fight — Anthony Ellot, the robber was, and
they hanged him the next year at Carlisle. . . . Hal
never could make me be 'Anthony Ellot.' . . . It's
a long story to tell, King David, and I'm a little
tired of talking . . . but the end was that Sir Lionel
got safe to General Monk—and *gave the message.*
If he had lost heart on the way, he could never
have given the message. And I must n't lose heart,
must I, till I give mine?"

Her voice ceased in sheer weariness. Tired King
David quickened his pace. Oh! for shelter, drink,
food for his darling, what could he not have borne!
He managed to stagger into the little yard before the
house, and seat Una upon a broken bench. And then
he knocked upon the door.

No answer. King David went around to the rear—
to find the place untenanted. The light he had seen

was a reflection of the setting sun upon a shattered pane! He climbed through a window, opened a door, and carried the child within. Rummaging the rooms, he found a quantity of clean straw with which he made for her a couch; and, lying there, her patient eyes followed the old man's movements lovingly. A well of clear water near the house supplied them with drink, and a bath for her wounded feet; and David had soon a bright fire crackling on the kitchen hearth. But food, whence was it to come? King David groaned within. Following out the well-path to a deserted garden, he smelt the rich fragrance of raspberries, and a cabbage-leaf full of these dainties was soon picked and eagerly enjoyed. Warmed by success, the old negro prowled off again into the now gathering darkness. Una heard a squawk of some feathered biped in distress, and immediately King David reappeared, bearing in triumph the mortal remains of a fine young fowl, captured upon the roost of a recently full hen-house.

It would have been hard to find any of the lower domestic arts in which David did not justify Mount Airy 'raisin'.' How he contrived it Una did not know, but ere long there he was by her side, holding a broken china plate, upon which smoked a morsel of broiled chicken, whose flavor was certainly beyond all criticism from her.

For safety's sake, he moved her bed to a room above, lying down across her door outside, with his head upon her valise. When her even breathing announced the girl asleep, the old man thanked God and fell himself into a doze.

Again the tramp of horses, late in the night. David, awake in an instant, crept to a front window and looked out. He saw a considerable body of cavalry draw rein below, and while their horses chafed upon their bits, heard the consultation of their officers.

"Empty as a last year's nest," said a voice that David knew, with a thrill, to be not one familiar to his native heath. And then a match flared out into the night, and he saw the Federal uniforms. "Nothing to be got here, that's plain, to help us to track the Johnny Rebs. Well, boys, we'll get along, and, luck helping us, be on their heels by daybreak."

They rode off in splendid style, and King David dozed no more. Early in the morning he aroused Una, and sharing the remainder of their food, the two set out again upon their weary way. How she was to endure another day's walk he could not tell; but in the refreshing cool of dawn they followed a wood-path for a couple of hours, emerging unexpectedly upon a spot where four roads met. Here a pleasant spectacle awaited them. Three ladies of gentle and kindly aspect were sitting on chairs on a farm-wagon piled high with household goods, to which a negro boy was engaged in harnessing a pair of stalwart mules that had been baiting on the way. Better than all, the ladies were breakfasting from an ample well-filled basket at their feet, and they cast upon Una a look of such compassionate astonishment as warmed poor David to the core.

"For gracious sake! what *is* that lovely child doing away off here with that old darky?" said the oldest of the three. "Come here, uncle, and give a

report of yourself. You don't belong hereabouts, I'll
wager a pretty penny; nor does she. Don't you
know better than to take her tramping about in the
track of the armies, eh?"

"We ain't no choice, madam," said David, with his
old-fashioned deference, standing hatless at the bar
of justice. "This here young lady is my little
mistis—Miss Una Eustis, of Mount Airy—and we
are on our way—"

"Eustis, of Mount Airy!" said the lady, letting fall
her knife and fork. "Why, child, your father is my
second cousin once removed. Did you never hear
him speak of his cousin Septimia Baskerville, of the
Bower? Come up here this minute, and get some
breakfast; and tell me if you dropped out of the
sky."

That Una's oft-repeated story brought moisture
into the eyes of her new-found relatives, we may be
sure. But Mrs. Baskerville was a cheery soul and,
above all, practical; and her first action was to see
both travelers comfortably fed, while her tongue
wagged incessantly in comment.

"Well! well! well! Wonders will never cease,
these war times. Girls, you have often heard me
speak of your cousin, poor dear Sainty Eustis—this
child has his mouth and eyes to a T. My child, if
I'd a roof to cover me, I'd take you under it and get
you started off with a proper escort. But we're refu-
geeing, as you see. Heard last night that our house
was threatened because my husband's a Confederate
brigadier, and started off at 3 A. M. Expect to sleep
to-night at my brother's, in the next county. We

are sure of one thing—the Yankee cavalry have just
passed down the road we 've got to travel. Here,
child, sit in my lap; and you squeeze in, old man,
somewhere beside Scip.

"Where 's my pistol now? Don't pack it with the
lunch. Bess and Jinnie—I never saw such girls!—
what *are* you laughin' at?"

"Another time, mother dear," said Bess, a young
person with many dimples, "when we set out to refu-
gee, if it 's all the same to you, I 'd rather leave the
ancestors at home. 'If it was n't for the honor of
the thing, I 'd just as soon have walked,' as the Irish-
man said when he rode in a sedan-chair without a
bottom."

"Yes, indeed, mother," chimed in Miss Jinnie, trying to keep her perch upon a miscellaneous pile of
picture-frames and furniture; "I 'm having a dreadful
time with great-grandpapa, who *will* hang over the
wheel. And as for old Aunt Dorothy, for a court
lady she 's positively ill-behaved. The only one of
them who lies low and gives no trouble is the Conti-
nental general, and he 's as good as gold."

"That Jinnie is a case," said Mrs. Baskerville,
smiling. "Could n't leave Aunt Dorothy, who 's a
genuine Vandyck, to be burned or to have holes
shot through her—could I, dear? Now, Scip, get
ahead, and make those mules travel till we 've turned
into the other road, where it is n't likely we 'll meet
the enemy."

Una, wondering, was taken to the hearts of these
brave women in a most consoling fashion. Her
limbs relaxed, and she slept most of the morning,

clasped in the arms of first one, then another; and
when she awoke it was to find the way beguiled by
quips and cranks of wit from the merry sisters, with
soothing assurances from their mother that, as far as
their ways lay together, she should know no want
or harm.   That age of enterprise, of endurance, of
common trouble, knit warm hearts into quick friend-
ships, and the Baskerville ladies had not often so
congenial an object for their sympathy.

Turned into a by-road, the mules proceeded leisurely; and late afternoon found our fugitives, after
a day without alarm, on the banks of a churning
mountain stream.

"Too bad! too bad!" said Mrs. Baskerville, surveying the situation with her keen blue eyes.   "As I
feared, the water's too high to cross, and we'll have
to camp under the evergreens yonder, off the road,
till morning.   Come, Scip, draw off into the pines,
and get the fly-tent up.   This old man is just the one
we needed, is n't he?   Somehow, things always happen
for the best, and it's a lovely evening, and no chance
of rain."

Under a fragrant roof of spruce and maple boughs,
couched upon waterproofs spread over a bed of
springy moss, Una spent her first night beneath the
stars.   Sharing "Cousin Septimia's" blankets, with
King David sleeping across her feet, she drifted off
into slumber happily, her last waking act to murmur
the lines her mother loved to say:

> And nightly pitch my moving tent
> A day's march nearer home.

Nearer home! Una was *at* home soon, through the witchery of dreams. Her father's arms were around her. Her mother sat there smiling. There was no war, and the grave, sweet face of Sir Lionel looked at her from his frame, a "well done" for her trust fulfilled. No war! Why, where, then, was Hal? No war! What was that sharp report ringing out upon the silence of the hour before the dawn? A crack, another, and yet another. Cries, oaths, groans, shot after shot riddling the trees around their hiding-place.

They knew by experience what it was. The Valley women were broad awake in a minute, their hearts beating fiercely, but calm and mistress of themselves. They held together behind the tree-trunks, the negroes at their knees. Hardly a word passed between them while the skirmish lasted.

And it was over wonderfully soon. The soldiers nearest them were evidently ambushed. There was the sound of horses plunging and struggling in the ford, and a Southern voice cried out:

"We 've missed 'em, boys. Ride to the upper ford, and head 'em off. We 'll save a mile and catch 'em yet, the varmints!"

Una clutched King David's arm. She had not noticed that the old man's body shielded hers.

"King David, that 's our lieutenant's voice."

"Sounds mons'ous like, honey. They must 'a' come here and hid, arter we fell asleepin'. God send they ain't any of 'em hurt."

Ere the clattering hoofs had ceased to echo, darkness had fled before the rosy touches of the dawn.

A strange light crept into the woods. They could see each other's faces, blanched and set. And the birds twittered in the joy of day returned.

"That *was* a narrow shave," said Mrs. Baskerville, looking critically at a bough cut by a Minié ball a foot above her head. Well, Scip, you 'd better harness up, right away. We 'll cross at the upper ford, and take the short cut to the other road."

"I heard groans, but I don't see any dead or wounded," said Bess, who had been absent on inspection of the outskirts of the camp. "Mother, I don't mind saying now that I 've had about enough of war."

Una, during the bustle of preparation, stole aside. She wanted for a moment to be alone with God.

It had grown brighter in the wood. A squirrel running down a tree stopped to stare at her. As he sped away Una's eyes followed him. And there, protruding from a clump of undergrowth, she saw a man's dead hand. There was no mistaking him. He lay flat upon his back, his huge bulk crushing down a bed of maidenhair ferns, his flannel shirt stained at the breast, his sightless eyes wide open. It was poor John Britton, self-devoted to be Una's "frend til deth."

.     .     .     .     .     .     .

No, this was no time to waver, when her feet were so near the bourn. Mrs. Baskerville, who cried over and kissed Una, and pleaded with her to come with them and wait for a safe chance to cross the Union line, could not shake the girl's resolve. The two travelers were still beating about from pillar to post, taking the fortune of the road, when the good lady and her daughters, with their impedimenta of ancestors and sundries, had been long installed in comfortable quarters. Many days were lost in planning for opportunities that never came to run the blockade. Their store of money was nearly exhausted, the month had passed away, and the flame of hope was flickering in the socket. Then Una declared she would press forward again on foot.

They set out through the ravaged country, where the flying crow had to carry his rations with him; and, after various adventures, were approaching the vicinity of Mount Airy, when, trudging along the highroad, they were overtaken by a body of Union cavalry, well mounted and equipped, whose debonair young captain, a-glitter with gold lace, pulled up at sight of them. His questions, sharp at first, grew gentle as the answers came, and seeing the girl's condition, he called out to an orderly to take her before him on his horse to a Dutch farmhouse a mile or two away.

"Rode two days with rebel scouts, you say?" he ended, with a laugh. "Well, when you get back again to Dixie, tell 'em that Uncle Sam's boys don't mean to be beat by them in taking care of the ladies, any more than with bayonets or sabers."

He rode off, touching his cap. Una had not seen so gaily caparisoned a cavalier since the war set in. Too worn to speak, she smiled her thanks to the orderly, who gathered her, lamb-fashion, to his breast, told her he had "a little 'un at home," and beguiled the way with stories, as the horse left King David far behind.

The Dutch farmer's wife, who gave them supper, a bed and the promise of a lift in an ox-cart the next day, smiled scornfully when she saw the Confederate money hoarded for this last expense. But she relented afterward and took it, to lay away in a stocking-leg as a memento of the war, perhaps; and the farmer's lad, who on the morrow guided his slow beasts hitched to a pole between four wheels, on which Una and King David could with difficulty maintain their balance, took them a good mile farther than the authorities at home had instructed him to go.

Now at last they knew themselves to be within but a few miles of home. But it was said that between them and Mount Airy stretched a blue cordon of Union troops, to cross which no wayfarers were allowed without a satisfactory account of themselves, and taking an oath of allegiance to the United States. Poor little Una drew the rags of her secessionism closer, as she thought of this. As a last hope, she determined with King David to present themselves *in forma pauperis* at the nearest Federal headquarters, and ask leave to go to seek her father. "I am not afraid of the Yankees," she said, "if they are all like that captain and the orderly who told me about his child at home." But King David was not so sure.

They had yet a mile to walk. The burning sun beat on the hot flints of the turnpike as she limped along in the old man's wake. It would have been hard to recognize in this thin, wan Una, with the

18

dark circles around her wistful eyes, the shabby frock and torn shoes, the fairy-beauty of her father's home. At last she put her hand to her brow, and, like the reaper's child of Scripture, cried out, "My head! my head!" and King David caught her, as she reeled, upon his breast. He bore her underneath a leafy bower, her golden hair drooping across his tatters, so tired himself by this additional exertion that, for a moment after laying her upon a bed of moss, he could only stand, catching his breath and wiping the mingled sweat and dust that poured down his wrinkled face.

"Even if I dared to leave her, there ain't no spring as I know on, hereabouts," David said to himself, forlornly, and in his extremity burst into tears.

"Why — King David," her soft voice said chidingly, "you 're not really crying? Crying for *me?* See, I am better already, since we 've come out of the sun. . . . If it had been Hal who was taking the message, he would n't have broken down. . . . Oh! I am sure those officers won't refuse to let me inside their lines. . . . Soldiers will surely not be angry with me because my father met them in fair fight and Hal was killed. . . . Maybe there 'll be one who 'll think about his own children, like my orderly; and he 'll understand how fathers and little daughters want each other . . . *dreadfully.*" She was silent for a while, crying quietly. David knew how much these rare tears meant. Never had he felt his ignorance, his lowliness, his impotence to shape events, as now. A keen sense of his stewardship to her absent parents oppressed his conscientious soul. Act he

must, but whither should he turn? Hobbling down
to the edge of the road, he strained his eyes up
and down its desert length.

What was yonder cloud of luminous vapor rolling
in from the direction whence they had come? That
wave of sound gathering strength and substance as
it reached his ear? King David gazed and prayed,
and presently, emerging from the golden mist, he saw,
first, horsemen pacing leisurely; then caissons and
guns, and after them rank upon rank of marching
men in gray. And above the dust, banners of scarlet
crossed with blue. And above the noise of tramping
feet, a chant arising, caught up along the line and
rendered with a grand sonorous swing:

"She breathes — she burns — she 'll come, she 'll come!
Maryland! My Maryland!"

A brave sight and a stirring one, wherever seen,
that of an army on the march! When the first de-
tachment of troops was called to a halt where the old
negro stood entranced, it became clear that, in spite
of feet bare and bleeding, faces flushed and eyes
bloodshot from the sun, patched garments white
with dust, and empty haversacks, some keen exhilaration nerved their ranks.

"I say, fellers, I don't know whether Maryland 's
a-burnin', but I 'm tarnation sure I be," cried out a
veteran, who thus easily produced a laugh among
his mates.

"Is there any little commission you 'd like us to
execute for you in Washington, old man?" one of

them remarked, with profuse civility, to the spell-
bound David. "Wrap yer compliments up in a neat
package, and I'll take care that President Lincoln
gets 'em safe."

"Perhaps you're traveling back Richmond way,
Brer Pompey," observed a third banterer. "If you
are, please call on Marse Jeff and tell him you saw
me on the way."

David turned, bewildered, to a soldier encircled with
a bristling array of kitchen implements, and carrying a posy on his bayonet.

"Which way air you goin', if I may make so bold,
sir ?"

"Well, Uncle, you *are* behind the times," the man
answered cheerily, "not to know we're part of
Early's corps marchin' on to Washington."

At this juncture, Una, fair as a star when only one
is shining in the sky, appeared on the bank above.
King David forgot everything beside, and in the
voice of a clarion shouted out:

"Do you hear that, my honey ? The good Lawd
has opened a way a-purpus for you to git to see
your pa!"

· · · · · ·

IT was a royal progress thenceforward. Some of
the officers, interesting themselves in her affair, voted
her straightway a seat on a caisson to finish her
journey with the corps. On this rude chariot, smoke-
stained with recent battles, wreathed with wood-
blossoms by the men, the little daughter of Mount
Airy forgot the sorrows of the way, forgot uncertain-

ties ahead, and, thrilling with pride and pleasure,
rode on the wave of an invading army to the very
gateway of her home.

Cheered to the echo by the soldiers, she remained
standing beside King David under the iron arch of
the outer gate at the entrance of the old familiar
avenue, till the glow of excitement faded with the
passing of the troops. Now, she was possessed by
an indefinable dread of disappointment to come,
and this she saw plainly mirrored in the old negro's
dog-like eyes that followed every expression of her
face. Neither dared breathe to the other the fear
that, ten chances to one, the journey had been made
in vain. King David thought of those many weary
miles to be traversed before he could restore his
treasure to her mother's arms; and in silence, almost
like culprits, they took their way along the grass-
grown avenue, through the pine-woods that con-
cealed the house from immediate view.

Dusk had fallen, and their first glimpse of the dwelling did not reassure the newcomers. Shutters were
closed over the double row of windows at the front;
moss and grass sprang from the crevices of the quaint
pyramidal flight of stone steps leading to the great
door whose very fan-light and side-lights were blocked
within. The long arms of oak trees swept the slated
roof as the breeze stirred them. A "little noiseless
noise among the leaves," the even-song of insects, was
the only sign of life that had made the place so dear.
Chilled and spiritless, the two stood for a moment on
the weedy carriage-sweep, gazing up. Then King
David's eyes spied a faint curl of smoke issue from

a pile of chimneys at the rear, and, brightening, he laid his hand upon the heavy knocker of the door.

"Oh! don't knock, King David," the child cried, turning whiter. "I 'm not ready to bear . . . disappointment yet."

"I reckon I 'd best go roun' to the back, honey," he said, himself glad of the respite.

When she heard the last of his halting movements, the child's physical courage for the first time failed. Trembling like a leaf, she dropped upon the upper step, with her cheek against the door. A cloud came upon her brain. She did not hear the turning of the big key in the lock; she knew only that she was lifted up and carried inside, to a room where a light was burning — that Mrs. Ryan had hold of one of her hands and was crying while she held water to her lips.

"Papa?" Una gasped, and was answered by King David's tender tones.

"Keep strong, my honey," the old man said, trembling strangely. "The Lawd, that 's bin our pillar of fire by night and of cloud by day, has given you your heart's desire."

The child sprang to her feet, every nerve strung, her face illumined with pure joy. Poor Mrs. Ryan, divided between anxiety for the worn little creature and a keen desire to confer instant happiness, knew not which way to look in answer to the searching of Una's eyes. Her own gaze appealed in turn to David, who nodded a joyful yes. Then the good woman took Una by the hand, and leading her down the long corridor to the study door, opened it and gently pushed the child within. The two eager listeners outside heard a low cry—another—a flutter as of a homing dove, and King David stretched forth his hand and closed the door.

"There ain't no ears but the Lawd's as ought to hear my little mistis give her message to her pa," he said, straightening his bowed form like a sentry on his post.

This and what followed is, by now, ancient history in the Old Dominion. The case of Colonel Henry St. George Eustis, of the Virginia Volunteers, who, struck by a bullet on the left side of his head at Gettysburg, received a depressed fracture of the skull which caused paralysis, with mouths of absolute loss of memory of words, and of inability either by speech or writing to convey to others any thought, is but one of many like cases in the annals of that time. It was through the good offices of the faithful overseer Ryan, who heard from his son the Union soldier that Colonel Eustis had been seen by him in a prisoner's hospital, that a cure was accomplished. Ryan had bethought him to make appeal to an old friend of the Eustis family before the war, in the dignified person of Secretary —— of the —— Department at Washington; who, bethinking him, in turn, of many pleasant weeks spent in boyhood as a recipient of Mount Airy hospitality, promptly made up his mind to see that the hapless prisoner had all the benefit of modern surgery before returning to the custody of his friends. An operation, performed successfully in a hospital at Washington about the latter part of May, just as Una had set forth upon her quest, had been communicated by letter to Mrs. Eustis in Virginia, and the prisoner was afterward allowed, on parole, to go to his own house, in charge of Ryan. Even as Una had crossed the threshold of her home, an order was on its way thither from the Bureau of Exchange of Prisoners, informing Colonel Eustis that he was to return by flag of truce to Richmond and to his wife, who was expecting him with a joy tempered only with anxiety for the welfare of their daughter.

.    .    .    .    .    .

THERE is a new portrait on the wall of the Mount Airy dining-room, facing that of Sir Lionel who "bore the message" long ago. It is of a brilliant, handsome lad, clad in a soldier's gray woolen shirt. Above it hangs a soldier's cap, wrapped with a bit of crape — a memento of his share in the war for Southern independence which Hal's mother cherishes. Below it is a picture of another soldier in the same uniform, in whose lineaments Mrs. Ryan, now the widowed housekeeper of Mount Airy, is proud to recognize and point out to visitors her second son, Dennis, who sleeps in Hollywood at Richmond. Bill Ryan, married and settled in place of his father as overseer of the Eustis estate, has supplied Mount Airy with another edition of Denny, in the person of his heir, long-legged and freckled-faced; and the second Denny has found playmates among the boys and girls born at the "great house" since the war. But under the honey-locusts in the Mount Airy graveyard rests the gentlest heart that ever beat with love for Una. Having seen his "little mistis" with the orange-blossoms in her hair, King David was satisfied to go.

www.ingramcontent.com/pod-product-compliance
Lightning Source LLC
Chambersburg PA
CBHW030119030726
47498CB00007B/2456